I0640117

To my strong and terrifying daughter

Princess Ambrosia
INTO THE DARKNESS

By: Neil Cohen

Written and Published for Chelsea's 13th birthday

Prologue

The kingdom had once stood on the brink of total annihilation. With the formidable Evil Wizard finally in possession of Princess Ambrosia's powerful magical ring, all had seemed lost.

Our heroic champions - the resilient Princess and her courageous friend Frankie the Firefly - refused to surrender.

In her earlier battles against the kingdom's darkest foes, Ambrosia's natural fearlessness and the support of her friends allowed her to prevail - even over the wickedest of witches and the Evil Wizard himself.

Then everything changed! With one surprising burst of rainbow magic from our brave Princess, she banished the Evil Wizard to the dreadful Badlands - ending his reign of terror.

Peace and harmony returned to the kingdom, shining like a beacon of light. While still discovering her newfound powers, Ambrosia ruled with confidence and joy.

But even in the brightest of light, evil and despair still lurk in the darkness…

Chapter 1

Once upon a time, in a kingdom far far away, there lived a beautiful Princess named Princess Ambrosia. Princess Ambrosia dressed all in rainbow. She had a rainbow dress and a rainbow skirt, she had rainbow socks and rainbow shoes. She wore a golden crown, but she had pink lipstick.

It was another sunny day at the castle as Ambrosia walked through her exquisite gardens. Without a care in the world, the Princess often spent her mornings treasuring the sweet aromas rising from the royal flower beds. Her gleaming smile twinkled as she would sift her hands through the tall green leaves feeling the morning dew between her fingertips.

It had been several months since the battle over the Badlands, and Ambrosia had come to embrace her destiny as the kingdom's powerful Princess. Living each day completely devoid of fear, she no longer looked over her shoulder for villainous witches or evil wizards.

Ambrosia chose to focus on moving past those horrific memories, and like any magical teenage girl, she enjoyed improving her conjuring skills.

Lying on the grass that morning, the short blades brushing up against her cheek, Ambrosia raised her hand in the air and cast a simple sparkler directly from her finger. She gleefully guided it high up in the sky until it suddenly whacked into the side of the castle walls.

"Oops!" she giggled.

The Princess was honing her powers but she still had difficulty controlling it.

She announced to herself, "Again!"

This time, with eyes closed, the sparkler grew in strength and eventually turned into a fiery pinkish flame. She felt the magic flow through her as she once again commanded the fireball upwards.

Ambrosia was really focused, her concentration giving her strength, but she suddenly heard a faint buzzing sound approach her. She raised one eye open just enough to notice a familiar face circling her above.

She perked up, "Frankie?"

The excitement of seeing an old friend was top of her mind, and she completely forgot about the plunging inferno she created as it smashed into the ground. The grass was set ablaze and Ambrosia gasped. She acted quickly and controlled the fire with a quick-thinking cooling spell, quenching the flames without causing too much damage.

"Sorry for startling you Princess," Frankie squeaked.

"Oh it's okay Frankie." The Princess was always excited to see her little firefly. "It's so good to see you!"

"You're getting pretty good with that magic. But please be careful, I don't want you or anybody else to get hurt."

The Princess stared at Frankie as if he had spoken a foreign language.

"Hurt? C'mon Frankie, I'm just having fun! Besides, I've got to practise my powers so I can take on the next threat to the kingdom!"

Frankie rolled his tiny eyes as he watched Ambrosia act out one of her usual imaginary scenes battling some fictitious monster.

"Princess, there hasn't been any trouble in a long time. You defeated the Evil Wizard; he isn't coming back. Let's go have some fun in the dark forest."

"Ohh fiiine!" Ambrosia uttered.

The Princess loved exploring the endless thick trees and coarse bushes in the dark forest. It added a small element of fear and risk mixed in with a quick shot of adrenaline that the Princess secretly missed. Frankie wanted to feel important as his belly shone the way through the notoriously darkened jungle.

It was a typical adventure for Ambrosia and her firefly as the two often played games, including hide-and-go-seek which was their favourite. Frankie always had the advantage of elevation and height, while the Princess occasionally cheated using her magic to detect little Frankie.

They would also try to find new areas of the dark forest hoping to come across something mystical or even a bit creepy. Rumours about the dangerous wildlife were often over-exaggerated; they had never found anything as intimidating as they hoped.

Ambrosia wanted to rest a bit, so she sat down by the trunk of a thick tree; Frankie landed on a low-hanging branch above her. Almost immediately, the tree's limbs began to shake.

"What the…?" and before Frankie could even finish, long prickly branches had begun to move and surround Princess Ambrosia.

"Princess!" Frankie yelled.

The branches wound tighter around Ambrosia; she was stuck. Frankie's worries began to ease as he noticed a rainbow light pulsing through the thick branches - until they exploded with a mighty force!

The Princess stood up with a proud look upon her face like a mighty champion. She noticed the other branches were still moving towards her, so she turned towards the savage tree.

Ambrosia sent a pulse of intense light from her outstretched arm towards the base of the tree, exploding it upon impact. The shock sent an immediate effect upwards, splitting the tree in two as it toppled to the ground. Branches were flailing everywhere and then it lay still, no longer moving.

"Whoah Princess, that was incredible!"

The Princess was glowing with pride. She had never displayed that kind of power before. It felt great!

"You okay Frankie?"

The firefly nodded and smiled at the Princess. "Of course, with you, we're always safe."

The two looked at the remains of the barbaric tree; kicking a few branches just to be sure it was no longer alive.

Then they noticed something odd on the ground where the tree once stood; an old wooden hatch that was firmly embedded in the dirt. The mysterious door appeared to be quite old, and had a black iron handle that was securely fastened.

It was also fairly large and Ambrosia could easily envision herself progressing through to a possible underground chamber.

Frankie and the Princess looked at each other with wonder and intrigue. This was a new kind of discovery for them and they were bursting with excitement.

The Princess smiled, "Shall we?"

Chapter 2

Frankie didn't even bother trying to convince Ambrosia otherwise. With her confidence level at an all-time high, there was no stopping her. The Princess didn't even wait for a response.

She grabbed at the cold metal and yanked at it with all her might. The door wouldn't budge. She tried again with a different technique, and really had a strong grip this time. She thought maybe she could get it loose by wiggling and pulling it as hard as she could - but still nothing! She collapsed on the ground breathing heavily.

Frankie piped up, "I don't think you're strong enough Ambrosia; it looks sealed tight. Maybe there's a good reason it's locked up."

But the Princess was determined, and often didn't listen to reason. She looked around and grabbed one of the sturdier branches nearby and approached the door with the intensity of a wildcat about to pounce on its prey. She was about to jam the thick branch in the handle, when she stopped.

"Wait a minute!" She threw the stick down. "Let me try a different way."

The Princess got on her knees in front of the door hatch, feeling the coarse wood with her hands. It was old. "Okay Frankie, don't move! And don't make a sound!" Ambrosia closed her eyes and concentrated.

Over the past few months, finding and harnessing her inner magical strength had taken quite a lot of practice -

and a lot of mistakes. But surprisingly, with no formal training, she had become quite the little sorceress.

Ambrosia had taught herself that an ultimate focus and having a strong-willed mind can result in more compelling magic.

Pushing hard on the hatch door, she felt a burst of energy flow through her entire body. She guided that strength and power until her hands began to glow. Frankie was always so impressed at Ambrosia's phenomenal abilities.

The ground began to shake, followed by the door which started to rattle; until the hatch opened with a loud pop!

Frankie yelled out, "You did it!!"

The Princess opened her eyes and grinned with excitement to see that a small opening had been created; a little bit of dust and smoke escaped outside.

Ambrosia quickly got up and with a good forceful tug; she was able to turn over the heavy door, dropping it backwards with a loud thud.

More powdery dust surfaced and they could see the black hole they'd opened up in the ground. They tried to look closely into the void but could see nothing except the top of what looked like a ladder going down.

Ambrosia was wild with excitement, motioning to Frankie. "You go first. Tell us what's down there."

Frankie's face initially dropped, but he knew that if there was a monstrous creature lurking below, his friend would save him.

Frankie flew down into the hole with his little light guiding him. His buzzing was quickly silenced as he descended further into the abyss, and it hadn't even been a minute and Ambrosia was getting impatient.

She whispered, "Frankie, you okay?" But her calls were unanswered. Again, this time a bit louder and with a little more concern and far less confidence in her voice.

"Frankie, tell me you're okay?"

Still nothing.

The Princess was getting anxious with a growing uneasy feeling in the pit of her stomach. Acting quickly, she snapped her fingers producing a small glowing torch hovering over her. Ambrosia commanded the bright light to lower itself into the cavern showcasing the remaining stairs of the ladder.

She proceeded to carefully descend down the steps. The ladder felt ancient and fragile and she herself was a bit jittery knowing Frankie could be hurt or in trouble. Only eight steps to reach the ground; which was good because her shaky muscles could not have handled much more.

It was cold, dark and damp with a whiff of musty decay in the air. She guided the luminous ball alongside her and she began to explore the underground chamber.

There wasn't much to see, just some rocks and sand. But she had only gone about ten feet inwards when her self-made torch revealed a dead-end. Ambrosia reached up to feel a rough wall made of slate and stone. She banged on it with the palm of her hand, testing for weaknesses - there were none.

She called out again "Frankie!" Nothing.

"Frankieeee!" Still nothing.

The Princess paused for a moment and grinned at her own brilliance, the ironic lightbulb above her head flashing. She quickly snapped her fingers to vanquish her beacon, the sound of which echoed into the hollow cave leaving her in a complete blackout.

Even at her young age, Ambrosia was mature beyond her years, feeling like she'd already experienced a full life. She was an accomplished interdimensional traveller, been chased by snakes, and repeatedly been tormented by vicious fanatics trying to steal her kingdom.

The Princess thrived on fear, but being blind and defenseless surrounded by complete darkness was a whole new challenge.

But her motives were full of genius, as what better way to find her glowing friend than by extinguishing all other light. She nervously looked around, hoping to glimpse the smallest luminescence Frankie might emit.

It wasn't necessarily the pitch blackness Ambrosia forced upon herself that spooked her, but it was more the emptiness and sheer silence that was unnerving.

The anticipation that something was watching her, or worse, would jump out at her from within the dark, was horrifying. She could hear the sound of her own heartbeat pumping rhythmically, her increasingly heavy breaths leading to even more panic.

Then she heard it!

It was faint at first, but the sound quickly escalated like a runaway freight train buzzing by her ears. Ambrosia let out a loud shriek and was left holding her chest as she saw Frankie circling her in the darkened room.

"Frankie!!! What the hell!"

Her palpitations began to subside as she was comforted by her tiny companion.

"I called and called; where were you? I got scared!"

Frankie looked at her with astonishment. "I didn't hear anything, but you gotta see what's in that room over there. It's incredible. So much stuff!"

Ambrosia perked up? "Room? What room? And what stuff? How did you even get in there?"

The Princess couldn't wait to turn the lights back on and she was getting quite good at showing off her magical abilities in illumination.

Frankie started to laugh. "Well you see, there's a small hole in the rock, and well, I'm small."

Ambrosia rolled her eyes. "That's great, but how am I supposed to get in. There must be a way!"

Ambrosia inspected the wall more intensely this time and indeed she could see where little Frankie had exited through some of the small crevices. She took a step back to examine the full blockage and noticed that this was no ordinary rock formation. It took the shape of a large door.

The Princess' eyes widened with excitement as she was eager to solve this mystery and continue the adventure on the other side. Ambrosia thought about using her magic but this door was extremely large, and she couldn't risk the ground above caving in on them.

"Frankie! Help me find a way to open this!"

The Princess began working quickly to examine every part of the cavern. She was so frantic and restless that Frankie could barely keep up. But he was more calm and meticulous with his search, and he spotted something unusual sticking out from the bottom of the wall.

"THERE!" Frankie shouted.

The Princess stopped in her tracks immediately and pivoted towards the small steel pedal protruding from the rock. She looked over at Frankie and they both nodded in agreement. Ambrosia pushed down hard with her rainbow shoes so the pedal reached all the way to the ground. The resulting noise from inside the walls was promising; the collective sound of the colliding medal was music to their ears.

Ambrosia pushed on the door a bit and she immediately noticed it was not as solid as before. She slapped her hands on the rock and using her legs as leverage pushed the sliding door across the dirt. The massive structure was extremely heavy, but she had just enough force to allow herself to squeeze on through to the mysterious other side.

She guided her conjured lantern further into the secret room revealing as much as possible.

"Whoah," she exclaimed!

Everything was full of dirt and dust, and the musty smell was nearly unbearable. The light exposed a small table in the corner with some old books and a brownish-reddish box on it. She picked up the box and gave it a shake. There was something inside.

She began to open it, but was interrupted when she noticed a gritty, yet disturbing painting on the rock wall. She walked over and proceeded to rub off the dirt and grime from the canvas. It wasn't long before she uncovered the full photo of an older couple staring back at her.

The man had remnants of a scar on his face with dark sunken eyes while the younger woman also had a cold stare and possessed an unusual jaw line - both were deeply disturbing.

Ambrosia grimaced at the picture, "That's just too creepy."

Frankie agreed, "Yeah, they look so sinister."

It was then she saw something in the corner by an old rocking chair that really piqued Ambrosia's interest, almost hypnotizing her. It was an old, shabby-looking teddy bear that had certainly seen better days.

She picked it up and gave it a good shake, patting it down to get all of the dust and dirt off its small shaggy fur. She looked into its innocent blackened jewelled eyes and she fell in love. "Oh she's so cute."

She also detected a black pendant under its chin and that too was filthy. It was a little chipped, but after rubbing it clean, she could make out the small print.

"Oh look, her name is RANA. So sweet. I'm gonna take you home with me, and I am never gonna let you go!"

Then she turned back to the red box. She opened it up and inside were two shimmering gold bracelets. These artefacts were in perfect condition and Ambrosia picked one up to examine every shiny bit of it.

It had interwoven gold streams wrapped tightly throughout the band. There was no clasp or anything, just a beautiful golden circle that the Princess became enamoured with.

"I'm taking this too, Frankie. It's really pretty."

With Rana held tightly under her right arm, she slid the first bracelet over her left hand as she admired its beauty. It was a bit loose, but she didn't mind - it looked exquisite.

Suddenly the bracelet snapped tightly over her wrist, her ball of light immediately extinguished and then everything went dark.

Chapter 3

Frankie's little tummy was all that lit up the small room. He could hear the Princess snapping her fingers vigorously trying to produce another magic fireball - but she could not.

"Frankie, something is wrong. Nothing's working!" She tugged and pulled at the gold bracelet trying to rip it off but it was firmly attached to her.

"Ambrosia, I think we should get out of here. I can lead the way."

The Princess' frustrations grew as she was unable to conjure even the simplest of spells. But with her only source of light already heading for the exit, she had no choice but to follow.

"Frankie, wait for me!" She squeezed through the narrow doorway with her teddy bear in hand, and ran towards the ladder.

Upon reaching the surface, she sat on the ground and sunk her head between her knees.

"What happened down there Princess?"

Ambrosia still needed to collect herself as she didn't want Frankie to see her sobbing. She took some breaths and finally showed him the bracelet.

"This happened Frankie!" Her voice cracking with a touch of hysteria. "I can't get the stupid thing off."

Again she tried to tear off the chain with all her might, but it was no use.

"I can't feel anything, I can't do anything. I think this bracelet is blocking my magic! I've lost all my powers!"

Ambrosia could not hold her emotions any longer, she took one look at Frankie and she burst into tears. Frankie was speechless. He didn't know what to say. But there was nothing to say. He wished they hadn't gone down there in the first place.

"Okay, um Princess. It's starting to get a bit late, so why don't we go home and we'll figure this out tomorrow."

Ambrosia wiped her teary face and nodded in agreement. She carefully closed the hatch and the two slowly headed back to her castle. There was little conversation between the two friends as they returned, with Ambrosia mostly preoccupied with her troublesome new trinket wrapped around her wrist.

"I'll see you tomorrow Frankie," the deflated Princess said as she approached her castle.

Ambrosia closed the door and shut her eyes tight, hoping and praying that this was all a big joke; that it simply wasn't real. But reality set in quickly as she could still feel the tight grip the mysterious bracelet had on her. She lay in her bed depressed and crying, firmly clutching Rana until eventually she passed out from exhaustion.

Princess Ambrosia woke swiftly as the sun's rays penetrated her room. Her eyes wide open, staring at the ceiling, she grabbed at her arm and could still feel the cold metal on her skin.

She walked outside but things looked and felt very different. The flowers in her garden had begun to wilt. As well, the trees surrounding the castle were deteriorating rapidly with crumpled leaves falling to the ground. The sun began to disappear behind incoming dark clouds that seemed to hover only over her castle.

Suddenly, the temperature began to plummet and she started to shiver.

Ambrosia was certain this was no regular storm or unusual weather but the work of some sinister magic – and that the bracelet was the cause. She could hear the rumbling of immense thunder in the distance and it shook the ground beneath her.

She thought about retreating back into her castle, but the selfless Princess wanted to check in on Frankie. She got to the edge of the dark forest and was taken aback at the swaying trees and howling noises coming from within.

Then she heard a faint whimpering cry that sounded like a wounded animal begging for help. She walked swiftly towards the awful noise, a terrible moaning sound that Ambrosia could only interpret to be suffering.

The cries grew louder and louder as she approached a large thorny bush to which she did not hesitate to rush through. As she entered, the prickly plant scraped her leg above the knee. But Ambrosia was so full of adrenaline she barely noticed.

Her chest beating hard and hands trembling, she reached the centre to pull back some leaves. Her eyes widened and her heart sank! She screamed to find Frankie lying on the ground in terrible pain!

The Princess' screams echoed in her head as she suddenly found herself back in her own room sweating profusely. She realized it had all been a terrible dream!

She immediately looked at her arm and was saddened to see the bracelet still affixed to her wrist; her stuffed little bear by her side.

"Frankie!" she shouted.

She hopped out of bed and ran outside. She barely even noticed her gardens, the trees, the skies; all normal. She sprinted into the dark forest calling for her firefly, hoping Frankie was okay. She had difficulty calming herself down as she frantically looked around the forest in a panicked frenzy.

"Hi Princess, what's wrong?" Frankie flew in by surprise.

"FRANKIE! You're okay?" Wiping the sweat from her brow, Ambrosia was relieved but exhausted.

Frankie couldn't even get a word in as Ambrosia's emotions continued to erupt. "I had the scariest dream I've ever had! The kingdom was in ruins, my flowers dead - and you! You, Frankie! Oh it was horrifying. You were crying and hurt and I was so upset."

He finally found a time to speak. "Well Princess, I'm okay, I'm here. I'm perfectly safe. It was just a bad dream."

He continued to console her but noticed she had a cut on her leg. "Oh you've hurt yourself Ambrosia?"

She stared at the thin red line which still had remnants of her fresh dried blood. The realization that her dream may be turning into a real-life nightmare hit Ambrosia especially hard.

She became dazed and began to blur everything else out, almost as if she was going into shock.

Frankie's loud humming wasn't helpful as it kept Ambrosia in her trance.

In a monotone voice she finally spoke out "That happened in my dream Frankie. It's all real."

Frankie could tell Ambrosia was in a state of confusion and began calming her. His squeaky voice slowly brought the Princess back to reality and once alert, she became extremely agitated. She screamed loudly at the sky; then proceeded to walk up to a tree and slam her left arm against the trunk trying to shatter the bracelet. Ambrosia winced in pain and was left more frustrated to see the shiny clasp still intact.

She began pacing back and forth clearly having her own private conversations while trying to decide what to do next. Frankie had never seen the Princess so irritable and with such rage. Even in her previous battles with the Evil Wizard, while he had seen her get angry and defiant, this was different; she was different.

He strongly suspected that this may be the work of darker magic, with the root cause coming from that cursed bracelet.

Feeling a bit shy and timid around his erratic friend, he finally spoke up. "Princess, maybe it's time we get some help? We can't do this alone."

Ambrosia looked at Frankie and with a kind of crooked smile, she replied, "Hmmm, I think you're right buddy. And I know just who to ask."

She hurried off back to the castle still with that peculiar grin on her face. Frankie followed her but she was already back outside by the time he got there. She had Rana with her and was already moving towards the forest with a sense of urgency in her step.

"Ambrosia, are you okay? Where are we going?" He rarely called her by her first name, so the Princess took notice and stopped.

"Well Frankie, we're going to visit an old friend. There's a small cabin deep into the woods. It's quite the trek; I hope you're up for it."

Frankie was relieved that Ambrosia was going to seek help and she already seemed like her old self again. He smiled and followed her into the dark forest where they began their long journey for answers.

Chapter 4

After a few hours into their expedition, Ambrosia needed a break. The blisters on her feet were accumulating and the scar on her leg was constantly stinging. Even though Ambrosia and Frankie had spent a lot of time together, they never really had a chance to talk openly.

"Princess, do you really think this is going to work?"

"Of course, silly," Ambrosia reassured her friend. "I've been in tougher situations than this."

He continued. "Okay, so let's say you get this curse lifted and you get your powers back, then what?"

She was confused at first at the question, but could tell Frankie wanted to have a real philosophical conversation. Ambrosia was exhausted so she manoeuvred herself against a tree. She grabbed her bear and got as comfortable as she could before responding.

"You know Frankie, I've never really thought of it. I mean I want to keep practising my magic because I need to be able to defend my kingdom."

"Okay Princess, but what if there are no more threats? What if those witches and wizards never come back? Then what will you do?"

The Princess was still young and quite naive, so of course she didn't have a plan. Combatting enchantments and fighting evil is all she's ever known. She certainly didn't know how to rule an entire kingdom.

"Well I don't know, but I still want to be prepared. What about you Frankie?"

"Well Princess, besides being devoted to you of course." The Princess responded with an adoring smile.

"I would like to know where I come from. Doesn't it seem strange that I'm the only talking firefly around here? And how did I get like this? Was I born here? Where is my family?"

Ambrosia interrupted, "Well silly, I'm your family."

Frankie grinned, "I know you are Princess, but I mean my real family. You have your magic and your kingdom and one day, you'll get married and become Queen. I can't expect you to hang around me forever. I don't even think fireflies live that long, but maybe I'm special. Well I know I'm special, but maybe I'd like something more than just being your little shining light."

It seemed that Frankie had been waiting quite a while to get all that off his tiny chest. The Princess had never known Frankie to be so profound, let alone that he was thinking about the past and the future. Ambrosia yawned again and closed her eyes.

"You know Frankie," she murmured as she began to drift asleep. "You are so special to me. When I get my powers back I'll help you. It'll be fun...."

Her voice started to trail off. "It'll be fun when I rip your wings off."

Frankie's eyes shot wide open, shocked by what he had thought he heard. He quickly flew high enough out of her reach and then looked down to see that she was fast asleep.

Did he hear that right? Did she really say it would be fun to 'rip his wings off'?

Frankie was terrified for his own safety, but he was also concerned for the Princess as the effects of the cursed bracelet could have been acting up again.

Sure enough, as he watched from above, the resting Princess began to twitch and shake in her sleep. Her body convulsing in an unusual way; she was definitely dreaming again.

Ambrosia opened her eyes but there was nothing to see. It was black everywhere and all she could feel was a disturbing chill running throughout her body.
She called out for Frankie but there was nothing but empty echoes. 'Oh no, another nightmare,' she figured as this place was too unusual to be real.

She tried to shut her eyes and even pinch herself, but she would not wake from this horror. The Princess reminded herself to be extra careful as any injury she

22

sustained in this realm could materialize in the real world.

She began to hear whispers in the dark, multiple voices that she could not make out. Then the sound of heavy breathing seemed to be approaching her from all sides. Without the ability to see, her heightened senses were on overload as the distressing noises put a fear in Ambrosia that she had never experienced.

Shaking and trembling in the pitch-black void, Ambrosia began to lose her mind. Her emotions switched quickly from fright to angst to fury, lashing out in the dark to anything that she thought approached her.

Her madness seemed to escalate and encourage the noises as the heavy breathing turned to loud growling. The sounds of murderous creatures could be heard in all directions and seemed to converge towards the Princess.

It was then she saw a flicker of light in the distance; a ray of hope that pulled Ambrosia out of her delusional state and gave her focus. As she inched closer towards the faint glow, the terrible sound of moaning began to increase.

The moans turned into screams and the Princess put her hands over her ears because the torment was overwhelming.

She stopped in her tracks to find Frankie lying on the ground in agony, his wings ripped off! Ambrosia shrieked hysterically and suddenly everything went bright. She was back in the forest resting by the tree still screaming in shock.

Frankie could see the distress his friend was in and immediately called from high atop the tree.

"Princess, are you okay? I think you had another bad dream."

The Princess was disoriented but the sound and sight of Frankie with his beautiful wings intact gave her much needed relief.

Still trying to catch her breath, "Oh my gosh Frankie, what a terrible nightmare. It was so dark, and those awful haunting noises, and you, you were in pain! I can't take much more of this."

Frankie wanted to console his friend but considering her manic state, he needed to be cautious and vigilant in case she turned against him.

"I'm okay, Princess. Let's get moving! The sooner we get help, the sooner this can all be over."

Nodding in agreement, the Princess wiped off her tears, picked up her bear and the two marched onwards.

Chapter 5

The trek through the forest certainly had taking its toll on the two adventurers. With Frankie constantly looking over his shoulder and Ambrosia fiercely fighting her inner demons, the last leg of the journey was full of tension.

Much to their relief, as they reached a clearing in the forest, they caught a first glimpse of an old-looking, broken-down cabin.

The house was creepy with an almost supernatural feel to it. The darkened roof had many missing shingles while the finish on the rest of the cabin had completely faded.

It was dull and grey and the entire area smelled of death with all the surrounding vegetation completely lifeless.

Some windows were boarded up, and as they approached the front porch, they noticed the path to the front door wasn't as inviting as they hoped. Much of the wooden planks were rotting away and they could hear the frequent chirping sounds of insects from inside the wood.

The Princess began to quietly tiptoe around the cabin hoping to find another way in. As she walked by a blacked-out window, she caught a flash of her reflection; but it was not her own! The vision of an older woman with dark sunken eyes and a menacing smile stuck in her head. But when she returned for a second look and stared, all she could see was her true mirror image.

Frankie broke the silence. "Do you see something Princess?"

After an awkward pause and still gazing at the window, she finally replied. "No. I thought I saw something; let's keep moving."

Either her mind was playing tricks or the vision she had was real; but regardless she did not want to give Frankie any more grief.

They made their way to the back of the cabin where they found an open door covered by a ripped-up screen. The Princess whispered, "Let's go in."

Ambrosia pulled back the screen carefully and slowly, but it released a loud creaking noise that made her and Frankie squirm. They slipped inside and were immediately hit with the harsh smell of mould that practically suffocated them.

The Princess' careful strides were not light enough as the floorboards squeaked and wobbled with her every step.

There wasn't much to the place except a few wooden chairs, plenty of cobwebs and a kitchen that looked like it had been condemned years ago. The place was certainly deserted, but there was one room with a closed door they had yet to uncover.

With a delicate touch, the Princess turned the shaky knob and the door began to open. The two friends looked at each other with more nerves and horror as they discovered stairs leading down to a dark basement.

"We might as well, we've already gone this far," the Princess said quietly.

She crept down the stairs ever so slowly, and while her movements were quiet, her loud breaths were not so subtle. Normally she was fearless. But with the bracelet restricting her magic, she had no way to defend herself. So descending into this type of unknown was well beyond Ambrosia's comfort level - she was afraid!

Upon reaching the bottom of the stairs, she noticed the room was almost bearable; especially compared to the abomination of the conditions above.

There were quite a few books lying around as well as a fireplace with a big iron pot. The Princess nervously explored the room and saw a small bed in the corner. With her back turned, she was suddenly startled by something grabbing her shoulder!

The Princess screamed with fright and turned to see a woman wearing a white cloak. The lady had hidden parts of her face, but the unmistakable shimmering emerald around her neck was a giveaway.

Ambrosia, still gathering her composure, blurted out "Midnight!"

The witch unveiled her cloak revealing her brilliant orange hair. Midnight was older than the Princess had remembered, but there was still much beauty hidden under that ragged facade.

"Well, well, well. Princess Ambrosia - and her teddy bear?" Looking up at the tiny glow buzzing in the air, Midnight continued. "Oh, and you must be Frankie?"

Frankie had heard many stories about Ambrosia's cursed pet tiger, but he had never met the real Midnight in person.

"Last I heard Princess, you finally rid yourself of that wizard. Rumour has it that you've also got some pretty nifty powers of your own."

Ambrosia perked up. "Yes! But that's why we're here! You see, Frankie and I went exploring and we found this secret underground bunker. It was incredible!"

Then she shoved her arm in Midnight's face. "And then I put THIS on my wrist. Now I've lost all my powers and I'm going crazy; and I'm having dark and scary nightmares. You have to help me!"

Midnight walked around Ambrosia looking her up and down. She continued to pace in circles around the Princess while remaining silent.

The tension in the room was high as both Frankie and Ambrosia hoped and prayed that the witch would help.

Finally she spoke. "You know Princess, I'm not going to lie; you do look a bit rough. Let's see this bracelet of yours."

She grabbed Ambrosia's arm and raised it to eye-level and examined it thoroughly.

"Ah yes, I've heard of these kinds of trinkets; they often come in pairs. In the past, they were used to imprison even the most gifted of sorcerers. I've never seen one in person, but they are powerful."

Frankie was incredibly grateful that Midnight knew what this was, but more eager for her to take it off the Princess. He interrupted. "So Midnight, can you get it off? I think it's cursed too."

Midnight turned around with a surprised look. "Oh look at that, he talks. Very interesting. And yes I think I have just the thing."

She placed one hand on Ambrosia's wrist, and the other on her green medallion; it then began to light up. Midnight mumbled some words in her head as Frankie and Ambrosia watched and listened intently.

Suddenly the bracelet clasp magically unlocked itself; Ambrosia quickly slipped it off and threw it in the corner of the room.

The Princess yelled with glee. "Oh my gosh it's off! Thank you, Midnight."

Immediately she snapped her fingers and produced a stunning display of rainbow light that danced all around the room. Frankie flew in circles as he was overjoyed for his dear friend but more so relieved that he was no longer in danger.

As the Princess walked around the small room testing out her magic, she noticed a cracked mirror leaning against the wall. She laid eyes on her reflection and once again, it was not her own and far more hideous and dreadful this time.

The more she stared, the more it enraged her. She screamed at it with a hellish fury and threw all her magical anger at it with destructive force. The crash shook the cabin as there were shards everywhere; Ambrosia was visibly irritable.

Midnight stared at her. "What was that? Why did you do that, Ambrosia?"

The shaken Princess apologized, explaining she saw something that scared her. All the commotion awoke Midnight's friendly orange cat out of hiding wiggling her way through her master's feet to investigate.

Princess Ambrosia's tone softened as she saw the feline. She smiled and nodded at Midnight acknowledging the twist of fate where ultimately she'd own a cat of her own.

The kitty approached Ambrosia and was taken aback! She began to hiss terribly at the Princess.

"Hey Jade, leave her alone," Midnight called out.

But her pet would not listen; instead Jade continued to be aggressive and agitated, her ears pulled back and she showed off her tiny fangs.

Midnight grabbed her kitty and had to pull her away while she scratched the floor.

"How about we all calm down, Princess? Why don't I make you something to drink? It will be good to catch up."

The Princess sat at the table while Midnight cooked some tea on the fireplace. Ambrosia looked around the cabin and although outer appearances looked grim, Midnight had really made a decent home.

Midnight sat down with Ambrosia and distracted her with small-talk while the Princess quickly sipped her warm drink.

"So, Princess, how are you?"

Neither of the girls had an abundance of opportunities for human contact, so this was much needed for both of them.

"I'm okay Midnight, just having a stressful day. What about you? I had heard stories that you were out here by yourself; but this place - this place is dreadful? Why don't you move to the village? I could help you get a much nicer place."

Midnight reached out and held Ambrosia's hand in hers.

"Thank you Princess, I mean it. But I'm better off alone out here. My kind does not mix well with the local townsfolk, and as you probably know, my family doesn't exactly have the best reputation."

"But it's so dirty and gloomy here! Why not make it bright and more pleasing? I could help!" The Princess was being really sincere.

"Ambrosia, that's really thoughtful, but honestly I'm so ashamed. What my sisters and I did to you was terrible and uncalled for. This is where I belong."

The Princess scowled, "Nonsense! At one point you and I were close - although you kinda walked on all fours. But still, I know you're not like Rubella or Cora - and I forgive you. Please! Come back with me and I'll tell everybody you're good. They have to listen to me, I'm the Princess! Also, I think we could both use a friend."

Midnight leaned back, "Okay I mean it's also not healthy or normal that you're hanging around with a firefly. I'll think about it, okay?"

The Princess was optimistic about resurrecting her relationship with Midnight, because it would be really great to have another sorceress in her life.

As she stared into her tea, her vision suddenly became blurred. She tried to speak but no words came out. She quickly became disoriented and everything was fuzzy including Midnight who was standing over her.

Ambrosia began to lose the feeling in her hands and feet until severe fatigue hit the Princess and she passed out.

"Princess!" Frankie swooped in to see if his friend was all right.

"Relax firefly, I just slipped some nutmeg into her tea, and maybe a special blend of sleeping potion. She'll be okay."

Frankie snapped at Midnight, "But why?"

"There is something wrong with our Princess, something terribly wrong! Jade can sense it. And that temper of hers is going to get us all killed if we're not careful."

She laid the Princess down on the bed, stuffed her raggedy bear by her side and began to study her motionless body.

Ambrosia did look peaceful at first, but Midnight was startled as her dormant legs started to shake.

"Oh no, she's dreaming again!" Frankie shouted out.

"Interesting," Midnight said again.

Frankie kept shouting with his sweet tiny voice.

"Why is everything interesting to you? Do

something! We took off the cursed bracelet so why isn't she better?"

Just then, Ambrosia's hands spasmed and she grabbed a firm hold of Midnight's arm. The orange-haired witch tried to pull free but the Princess's grip was too strong. The skin around Midnight's wrist began to burn as if Ambrosia was branding her. Midnight grimaced in pain and finally wrestled herself away from the Princess' clutches; but the damage was done. Most of the skin above Midnight's hand had been badly burned by Ambrosia's touch.

Frankie watched in horror as his beloved Princess groaned and grunted and battled and fought this destructive curse cast upon her. Midnight was in obvious pain but with one touch of her emerald, her skin magically started to heal.

Just then, Ambrosia awoke suddenly from her slumber and immediately began coughing and wheezing like she was out of breath. Trembling with fear, she curled up on the bed and needed time to recover.

Midnight whispered closely to Frankie, "This is very powerful evil, I can't stop this."

Frankie was beside himself. "What are we going to do then?"

She sighed. "There is only one person I know with enough wisdom and strong magic to defeat this!"

Frankie blurted out! "NO! You don't mean…?" Midnight nodded.

"But how? He is in the Badlands. How would we even get there? And why would we ever want his help?"

Midnight cracked a smile. "Oh there is a way my petite friend. And this may be the only chance we have to save your Princess."

Ambrosia had been eavesdropping and hopped out of bed with a great sense of determination. "All right, I'm in!"

Midnight and Frankie both looked at her in astonishment.

"Hey! I want these visions to stop! And I have my magic back now, so I can handle anything! What do we have to do?"

Midnight looked into the Princess' eyes and recognized her pledge and sincerity to get help.

"Okay, but I have to warn you both right now. The Badlands is a VERY treacherous and dangerous place. You've got to be totally committed!"

Ambrosia and Frankie had never backed down from a fight and were certainly not the type to avoid adventure. They both looked at Midnight and nodded in agreement. They were ready!

"Yes!" Midnight clapped her hands. "Let's begin!"

Chapter 6

Having been a seasoned witch for some time, Midnight had all the right elements to pull this off. She had never summoned a gateway before, let alone anything of this magnitude, but she wasn't about to let her companions know that this would be her first.

However, the cautionary speech about the Badlands - that was not a lie. When Midnight and her sisters were young, their mother Rubella used to threaten them with banishment to the Badlands if they misbehaved.

After feeding little Jade, Midnight took out a large book of incantations from under the bed. It had originally belonged to her older sister, but luckily Midnight had previously familiarized herself with its contents.

She flipped to the section about portals and dimension doorways and began skimming the pages to understand the appropriate spell.

Frankie and Ambrosia watched intently as Midnight began lighting candles at the table while still focused on the fine print within her grimoire.

"Hmmm interesting," Midnight said softly while Frankie rolled his eyes.

Then he spoke up. "Wait a minute! We're just going to stroll into the Badlands, find the Evil Wizard, demand he help the Princess, and then we're just going to come back and leave him there?"

Midnight slammed the book shut, almost crushing the little insect. "Exactly!"

Midnight explained with a devilish grin, "The gateway we create will be an Absolute Magical Portal."

She stated that with such confidence and satisfaction, but Ambrosia and Frankie looked at each other with complete cluelessness.

"Must I explain everything? Fine! It means if three go through the portal, absolutely only three can return. So when we find the Evil Wizard, we ask him to fix the Princess. In return, we 'promise' to bring him back. And then as soon as the three of us walk through the doorway back to our world, it will absolutely close on his old bony face, ha ha ha!"

Frankie chuckled to himself. "Oooh I like that plan. It's so 'interesting'."

Midnight and Frankie were really starting to get along. Ambrosia however was getting impatient and started pressuring Midnight to speed things along.

Sitting at a small table across from each other, Midnight began the spell with a touch of her gemmed necklace.

Midnight called out. "Take my hands Ambrosia. We're going to need some of that raw power of yours."

Frankie inquired, "So what's my job?"

"Don't worry little guy," assured Midnight. "We'll need you too. Everything in witchcraft requires three."

"But I can't do any magic."

"Well you are a talking firefly, so I have faith that you have something special to give."

Frankie had never thought of that before.

The idea of having a hint of supernatural abilities only furthered his fascinations.

Midnight continued to lead, "Now hover between us girls, our powers will fuel your light and open the gateway."

Frankie didn't question anymore, he was bursting with pride and pushed out his bright tummy to help complete the chain.

With their hands now locked together, both girls thrust their power outwards creating a shimmering white glow. Midnight softly began to recite the spell.

I call upon the great witches
Please give us the power
We need your strength
In our darkest hour

I call upon the great witches
Please protect this mortal
We need your strength
To open up this portal

I call upon the great witches
Please join our locked hands
We need your strength
To guide us to the Badlands

As the table and chairs began to shake, the candles flickered vigorously forcing poor Jade to scurry away in hiding.

The girls' blinding light launched upwards and connected with Frankie's radiant body resulting in a pulsing white orb that grew right in Midnight's living room.

Midnight severed the link and the three turned to stare at the magical doorway they had built. Frankie was in disbelief at what he helped create and reveled in the fact that his curious origins may indeed be magical in nature.

The sound emanating from the epicentre of the portal was deafening as the inter-world vibrations shook the room.

Midnight stood up and announced. "It's time. Are you both ready?"

Frankie was all pumped up now exuding confidence and ready to save the Princess.

Ambrosia called out "Can I bring Rana? She protects me. That doesn't count for the '3 thing' right?"

Midnight rolled her eyes and gave her a sarcastic 'thumbs up'; reminding herself that Princess Ambrosia was still very young. She often looked at the troubled girl with a motherly fondness and wondered if maybe she'd make a good role model for the Princess when this was all over.

Midnight grabbed Ambrosia's hand and the two looked up at Frankie. The Princess' heart raced as the three entered into the Absolute Portal and vanished!

Chapter 7

Over a century before our three heroes risked their life to venture into the underbelly of hell, the sound of adolescent laughter echoed through the cobblestone walkways near a small village in the Kingdom of Dysteria.

The vast land was ruled by a rich monarchy which was generous and quite loved by its people. Two childhood friends, both of magical descent, were often seen together causing mischief as teenagers often do.

Rubella was the younger of the two, a tall lanky girl with long brown hair. She had huge ambitions with excellent conjuring skills that often resulted in destructive consequences.

Fortunately she would always be protected by her high-born parents who consistently defended her. Coming from a long bloodline of witches, she represented the future of the family.

Astarroth was three years her senior and a far more skilled sorcerer. While slightly shorter and a tad heavier than his female counterpart, his dedication to the mystic arts was unprecedented and Rubella was secretly jealous of his power.

He had inherited most of his skills from his father, widely recognized as one of the most powerful warlocks that had ever lived.

As good as Astarroth had become, he always felt like he was overshadowed and ignored because of the successes of his superior father.

The two friends would often meet up in the local abandoned quarry where damage and destruction could be confined. Astarroth enjoyed practising the more advanced arts such as transformation and teleportation while Rubella was always interested in the darker side of magic.

One fateful day, Rubella had brought along some home-made hex bags and some potions that she had purposely overstuffed with explosive power. She planned to throw them at Astarroth while he'd attempt to teleport - giving him a good scare.

However with just the first bottle, he barely escaped the massive explosion; it nearly killed him. The blast was much bigger than Rubella had envisioned and could already sense she would be in trouble.

When the smoke and dust finally faded away, the two noticed a large chest sticking out of the dirt at the bottom of the newly created canyon. Rubella's eyes widened and she was the first to slide down.

"Come help me pull this out!"

Astarroth quickly followed and the two pulled the sizable trunk to the bottom of the large hole.

The mysterious deep-brown box had brass bolts lined up and down the front. It had a very eerie feel to it with three golden rings embedded in the mouths of lion heads. It also had a simple lock mechanism that the young warlock Astarroth had no problems picking.

They opened the chest ever so slowly. Peering inside they found an ancient book and a large black crystal ball.

The book was very old and difficult to open but they managed to break the seal. The script was new to Rubella who couldn't make sense of any of it. Astarroth however had seen similar writings from his father's work and had a suspicion about what they had found.

"Oh my! I think I know what this is. This is the original spellbook and crystal ball from the very first wizards and witches. This is beyond anything I've ever seen. I need to bring this to my dad."

Rubella punched him in the shoulder. "Are you crazy? We found it. You and I. It's ours."

Astarroth shook his head, "I don't know. This is extremely dark magic here."

Rubella punched him again.

"You want to show everyone how powerful you are; even more than your old man? This is your chance! Look, we're all the way out here, nobody will get hurt. We'll just do one spell. I promise!"

Astarroth reluctantly agreed.

They carefully flipped the pages of the sacred book trying to determine which enchantment to use. He called out the spells as he interpreted the scripture.

"This one casts a curse turning anybody you want into an animal. Ummm, this one..whoah! You have the power to control the spirit world." Rubella was awestruck.

The next was associated to a weird symbol. Astarroth skimmed through the text. "Oh this one will make you young again. We don't need that."

On the very next page, Astarroth put his hand to his mouth, "Oh my!" Rubella perked up, as the young wizard quickly turned the page. "That one was crazy. It says you can disintegrate your enemy by turning them into dust!"

Just thinking of the possibilities, Rubella was even more intrigued with these spells. She hoped to take the book home later.

They continued scanning until Rubella took a liking to a page; she felt it bonded to her. "Ooh Astarroth, let's do this one. What's it say?"

Astarroth began reading the passage to try and understand the spell. He was still inexperienced at translating the book's ancient language and this particular text was quite challenging. "Hmmm, I'm not sure, but I think it says you have the power to make it dark."

"Really? Let's do that one! We'll do it just over the quarry. Nobody will know."

While slightly hesitant to wield such powerful magic, Astarroth could sense the intensity and excitement in his female friend. It had always been difficult to say no to Rubella – especially when she was so persistent.

"Okay, it says here you need to keep your hands on the crystal ball at all times," to which Rubella quickly complied with such devious pleasure.

"Oh it also says we have to bind it with blood." Without hesitation, Rubella stuck out her palm like an eager child at Halloween. Astarroth pulled out his small dagger and first carved a bloody line across his own hand, gritting his teeth at the searing pain. He then obliged Rubella who didn't even flinch; she almost seemed to enjoy it.

Still in discomfort, Astarroth tossed the dagger aside and placed his hands on the book and began to read.

"vor dem bittet morana seco vivia elos caza"

The black crystal ball began to spin in Rubella's hands as she watched with wonder. The ground beneath them began to crack and a thick dark smoke rose above them. Astarroth felt nauseous as the smoke seemed to thrust through him, penetrating his soul. He released the grip on the book and unbeknownst to him, the smoke passed itself onto the nearest object - his dagger.

He looked on in horror where, next to him, more smoke had surrounded Rubella, seemingly entering her ears and out through her nose.

"Let go of the ball Rubella!" he yelled.

She held on long enough for her blackened eyes to fixate on Astarroth. As her stone-cold face etched in the back of his mind, he felt the presence of pure evil staring at him. She leaned over and whispered something in his ear that scared him senseless.

Finally she came to and released the crystal ball. The leftover mist had no choice but to secretly bind to the nearest object - one of Rubella's hex bags.

Then everything went still.

"Whoah. That was intense!" Rubella said with delight. Her demeanour was different; Astarroth couldn't identify it but felt she was smug and almost soulless.

"Yeah, I think we almost died there. We have to bury this chest so nobody finds it!" He could sense Rubella was not in agreement with him, but surprisingly she concurred.

The two set the chest down in the middle of the crater as they stood over it from a distance. Using both of their combined magic, they covered the pit with dirt until the box was sealed.

Knowing his friend's curious and devious nature, and now with even more distrust, Astarroth at the last second used his powers to teleport the chest somewhere secret - where he hoped she would never unearth it.

That was the last time Astarroth and Rubella went to the quarry and they never spoke of that incident again.

Chapter 8

Frankie was the first through to the other side and he immediately felt sick to his stomach at the stench of rot and death in the air. The sound and erratic movement of the roaring trees was terrifying.

Ambrosia and Midnight joined soon after and they almost slipped on the uneven ground encased in slippery mud. The low dense fog that had come in was suffocating and the grey skies above them were full of gloom and despair. As they continued to explore their surroundings, a light sprinkling of ash began to fall from the hellish atmosphere.

As one would expect, the Princess lacked restraint in this new world. She was the first to ensure her powers were at full capacity by illuminating the path ahead of them.

Midnight shot out at her quietly, "Hey, no powers Princess! We don't want to bring any unwanted attention!"

Ambrosia strangely snapped back. "Don't tell me what to do with my powers!"

Midnight had almost forgotten that the Princess was under the influence of a certain evil and reminded herself again to tread lightly.

She also wondered if the hatefulness contained in the Badlands was accelerating and perhaps worsening her condition.

The Princess returned to reality when she noticed two rodent-like creatures watching them from a nearby hill. They were only the size of a house cat, but black as coal brandishing razor sharp claws as well as menacing scorpion-like tails.

"Guys, let's get out of here," Frankie urged them.

They hurried by the creatures and continued along the swampy path until the rock formations frightenedly narrowed. Frankie had no problem flying through, but it was going to be an extremely tight fit for Midnight and Ambrosia. If anything or anyone was to attack them while they attempted to squeeze through, they'd be easy prey.

Midnight was the braver of the two as she nominated herself to go first. As she inched her way through the cramped crevice, the feeling of the slimy wall up against her face was almost unbearable. It was difficult to navigate, and half way through she had to hunch over and crawl through the tiny opening. She made it through with only a few scrapes and called out to the Princess to let her know she was safe.

Ambrosia began her crossing, but was very uncomfortable being so compacted against the rock. The Princess reached a point where she got stuck and immediately began to panic. It also didn't help that she refused to leave her stuffed bear behind. The girl with the filthy rainbow dress was now frozen with fear as she called out for help.

Midnight wanted to go back for her but was stopped in her tracks when she saw the walls had begun to move.

At first she thought it was an illusion, but under closer inspection she realized it was actually a large colony of angry red ants - and they were headed right for Ambrosia. These vermin had been known in the Badlands to devour large beasts in a matter of minutes.

Midnight called out to warn her distressed companion. "Princess, you have to hurry, there's an army of killer ants headed your way!"

Ambrosia yelled back. "What? Noo! I can't move. Make them go away!"

The Princess managed to lift her neck up just enough to see that the swarm of pests was almost upon her.

She sucked in her stomach and wiggled herself like a contortionist to get as low as possible. She began to slither through the slim opening but those insects were fast and surprisingly loud. Their clicking and chomping sounds bounced off the rock walls making it impossible for Ambrosia to determine how close she was to being ravaged.

The Princess could finally see Midnight on the other side and they tried to reach for each other with their outstretched hands. Their fingers touched but they could not obtain a strong connection.

Suddenly she could feel a slight tingling on the back of her legs as the first of the ants settled. She screamed in terror as she tried to manoeuvre herself through. But she was still stuck and Midnight could not get a firm grip to assist.

As more ants started to accumulate, they began to gnaw on her skin causing the pain to be unbearable. It felt as if her legs were on fire. She tried to shake them off, but it only made the ants more violent. Their insatiable thirst for blood continued as they slowly and gruesomely chewed away at her flesh. Ambrosia screamed in agony as tears began rolling down her cheek. The Princess nearly passed out from the pain, but much to her surprise, the torture surprisingly subsided.

The ants began to follow a small yellow light being led away from Ambrosia. It was brave little Frankie as he used his light to guide the bugs out of the passageway giving Midnight enough time to pull Ambrosia through safely.

The Princess was exhausted and traumatized as she sobbed on the ground. She looked down at her bloody knees double-checking there were no more bugs. There was one lone straggler who tried to scurry away. But it soon regretted not following his colony as the Princess savagely stomped on the ant with all her might. Her revenge and rage felt good as she seemed to enjoy squashing the killer bug.

Midnight felt the need to intervene and placed one hand on Ambrosia and the other on her own emerald. Her jewel shimmered as she slowly began to heal the Princess. Ambrosia was so grateful to have such courageous and helpful friends.

Their restrictive trek through the mountain did have its reward as it led them to the edge of a huge cliff with a majestic view of the Badlands. It was a great lookout point to survey the vast destructive wasteland of this suffering purgatory.

Off into the distance they could hear the awful and frightening sounds of larger creatures, their growls like thunder, as well as the squeals of others dying in agonizing pain.

Midnight was speechless as her perspective of this dark underworld had already exceeded her fears and expectations. This was a magnitude of hell she would not inflict even on her worst enemies.

Rain began to fall as Midnight and Frankie turned to go get cover. The Princess however refused to leave, almost fixated on the beauty of the abomination that was the Badlands.

She called out, "This place was in my dreams, I know it." The words rang in Frankie's ears sending chills down his spine.

"I think I'm meant to be here," she continued.

Midnight looked at Frankie and they both knew they were running out of time to save her.

Water and mud began to accumulate and suddenly the ground crumbled beneath the Princess; she fell several feet below. Frankie sprung into action and was the first to fly to the bottom.

Midnight slowly levitated down, surprisingly to find the Princess only with a few scrapes and still sporting a smile. Almost nothing seemed to faze her; not the rain, the ash, or even her ruined mud-soaked rainbow dress.

They stood before the mouth of a cave and Ambrosia called out, "I think we're going this way now."

Midnight and Frankie looked at each other and couldn't find any reason to challenge the Princess so they followed.

Before heading in, Midnight motioned the firefly to come closer as she touched her charmed necklace to intensify his little light.

"This should help us. Any reason for Ambrosia not to use her powers is a good one. We don't need to alert the entire Badlands of our presence." Frankie felt so mighty in that moment; he quickly led the way.

The cave was dark, damp and impressively large with giant jagged rock formations coming down from its ceiling. They tried to be silent, but the muddy ground soon changed to loud crunching noises.

At first they thought it was sticks or leaves, but Midnight was the first to notice they were stepping on piles of bones. They stopped to inspect the heap of animal remains when they heard they were not alone. The sound of heavy footsteps and a low-pitched growl trailed behind them.

Ambrosia turned around ready for a fight, but Midnight grabbed her hand and pulled her close to the wall. Frankie flew and hid behind them so they'd block his glimmering beacon. There was still enough light that they could make out the creature coming towards them.

Even though it walked on all fours, this apex predator was gigantic in size. This killing machine had large spikes protruding from its back as well as razor-sharp claws that could eviscerate its prey in seconds. His barbed tail dragged behind him, but the large black stinger at the end was perhaps its greatest weapon. It had an unusually small head for an animal this size but its beady green eyes and insanely sharp teeth only added to his menacing appearance.

The creature had a strong sense of smell and began to move slowly towards the three intruders.

Midnight whispered, "If it gets any closer, I think we have to run for it."

It let out a horrendous roar in their direction and Frankie shivered with fright.

"GO!" Midnight yelled as the three scampered deeper into the cave. The creature whipped its mighty tail against the rock, nearly decapitating the girls.

They ran as fast as they could, but the Princess slipped and dropped Rana on the ground.

"Keep going!" Midnight yelled.

But Ambrosia did not listen; she needed to go back and fetch her stuffed animal. She looked up to find the creature's massive body towering over her blasting his thunderous growls in her face. Midnight tried to pull the Princess away but Ambrosia stood her ground defiantly and readied herself to fight the creature.

She confidently raised her arm high with the plan to slay the beast with an epic display of magic - but nothing came out. There was no rainbow, no fireball, nothing! She tried again and again, but still came up empty.

"Oh no, not again! What's wrong?"

Midnight grabbed her emerald and aimed it at the creature, but she too had no magical ammunition.

"I don't know. I can't do anything either."

The cave monster took a mighty swipe with its lethal claws but the girls ducked and fell backwards. On the ground they started their slow retreat and could feel their impending demise as they hugged each other tightly.

They could feel the beast's drool and hot breath on their faces as it moved in for the kill.

Frankie called out, "Oh my..."

Suddenly the growls were silenced as thick blood spurted from its torso covering Midnight and the Princess.

A large spear had penetrated its body from behind sending the creature into complete anguish. The monster's dangerous tail still twitched and jerked as the beast flopped over and quickly perished.

Ambrosia and Midnight were in complete shock. They were trying to recover from the intense fear and also trying to navigate through their blood-soaked hair. The Princess slowly got to her feet, staring down the corpse of the creature that nearly gutted her.

But it was Midnight who first recognized their saviour standing before them - it was the Evil Wizard!

Chapter 9

It had been many years since the incident at the quarry but Dysteria had still remained peaceful and prosperous. A new king and queen had been recently crowned and with the passing of Astarroth's father, he was granted the position of Royal Advisor by the new monarchy. The wizard enjoyed his reclusive lifestyle but often visited the castle to perform his sworn duties.

The village hadn't changed much as one could always hear the sounds of the next generation of young people laughing and scheming. The town square was a popular and bustling marketplace where local workers and farmers could mingle and children could play.

Like many class-based settlements of its kind, there were great opportunities to flourish as well as those subject to hardships like crime and poverty. Magic was revered but not commonplace amongst the residents. With the exception of those with incredible powers, many kept it secret.

At its centre was the local pub which had always been the town's popular watering hole for years. One could find characters of all walks of life coming through those doors. It was a casual place where strangers could become friends and business deals of all kinds could be made.

One cool summer night, a man sat alone at a table sipping a hot drink. He was tall and lean, with a bit of scruff on his face. He kept up a lonely and depressing appearance but behind that innocent facade was that of mischief and confidence. As someone came by to refill his drink, the man cunningly - and magically - picked the waiter's pocket relieving him of his tips.

The man continued to drink with a proud smirk on his face when he was suddenly joined by an older woman.

"Wonderful job my boy. You've got talent."

The man looked surprised and was trying to respond with something clever, but came up empty.

"Don't deny it. But don't worry. I won't tell."

The man looked relieved but still felt uncomfortable with his new guest.

The lady tried to introduce herself, "My name is…," but he interrupted her.

"I know who you are. You're Rubella."

Everybody knew the great witch. Her magical abilities were legendary and everybody in town feared her. She was mean-spirited and ruthless and there had been rumours that she had tortured and slaughtered her own parents.

"Ahem. I am the oldest witch in my family, so you will address me as Queen Rubella."

The man gulped and hoped the old lady would leave him alone, but she pressed on.

"So you seem to know who I am. But I also know a lot about you. Viktor is it? You've got a pretty wife and a baby on the way. Money is tough so you come here to use your powers to make a little extra. Am I right?"

The man was speechless, he knew she was right.

"Well my boy, today is your lucky day. I've got a job for you. It should be simple for a slick thief such as yourself. I'll pay you well."

Viktor leaned back and listened, his obvious demeanour was that of curiosity and excitement; he needed the money.

"There is an older man - very good with magic - who lives near you."

This got Viktor's attention right away and just before he blurted his name out, she barked. "DON'T say his name! I don't want to hear it! But we both know who I'm talking about."

He nodded.

"Now he has something of mine and I want it back. And YOU are going to get it for me."

While the man was normally quite smooth and cocky, he was petrified of Rubella and quick to be obedient.

He timidly asked, "What is it?"

"It's a small dark chest, about this big. It has three lion heads on the outside; it's very distinguished. I know he has it stashed away in that house of his, and you my boy are going to steal it and bring it to me."

Again Viktor was about to speak, but she was quick to muzzle him.

"Don't ask what's inside! Don't look inside! Just bring the chest to me."

Viktor rubbed his short beard and pondered the job offer. The self-appointed Queen could tell he was still hesitant. She finally let him speak.

"Stealing from the old man is not going to be easy. He's extremely powerful. Are you sure you have the right guy for this?"

Rubella leaned in closer to Viktor. "Listen up my boy. You will soon be a father and have your own family to support. I have three bratty witches at home, I know. I'm sure you've also seen how difficult it can be to raise children in this world. I mean, look at your brother."

Viktor held his breath. "But, but how do you know?"

She quickly silenced him by putting her finger on his lips. "I'm Queen Rubella! I know everything." Her pompous and self-absorbed smile made Viktor feel so insignificant.

"I'm fully aware of you and your magical kin. You and your bloodline have some talent, but you waste it by stealing pennies. What I'm offering is riches beyond your wildest dreams."

She was right about everything; his family was gifted with magical abilities. But over the years, many of his relatives had squandered their talents and often fell into misfortune.

The job would not be easy; and while Viktor was more of an accomplished pickpocket than a house burglar, he felt he was up to the task. He also knew it was his best chance to finally make a name for himself and provide for his family.

Viktor agreed; but it was as if he was shaking hands with the devil. Knowing the witch's reputation, he also felt that he didn't have much choice. Nobody says no to Rubella!

Getting home to his wife Lara that night, he chose not to burden her with this new job opportunity tasked to him by the old witch. Instead he lay in bed waiting for his wife to fall asleep while he planned and plotted his upcoming heist. Viktor felt the ideal time would be to pounce that night while the old man slept.

With the late-night moon covered by clouds, Viktor quietly snuck out of his run-down cottage and headed towards his prize. As he crouched in the tall grass, he noticed the old man's wooden fence was not very high; making it an easy hurdle for Viktor. He quickly dashed towards one of the nearest windows and crept underneath trying to stay hidden.

His mind wandered a lot in that moment, his heart-rate rising dramatically, he wondered about the curious contents of the chest. He pressured himself to keep his focus, so he gathered his confidence and took several deep breaths before moving in.

Using a simple magic spell he guided the window up slowly, just enough for his lean body to squeeze through. He smoothly made his way inside and found himself in the old man's den. The farmhouse was quiet except for the loud snoring coming from the next room.

Viktor scanned the extremely messy office and soon began to regret his task. There were open spellbooks scattered throughout, and countless little potion bottles that conjured who-knows-what.

Even if he was able to find the chest amongst the chaos, it would be difficult to do it quietly. But an accomplished thief like Viktor was far more clever than most. He presumed that a prized item that piqued Queen Rubella's interest would not be in plain sight.

So he took one more careful look around the room specifically looking for secret compartments or trap doors. Nothing looked out of the ordinary until he noticed something peculiar in the centre of the ceiling, a potential spot for a hidden chamber.

He softly navigated across the room to the old man's desk to find something that would crack it open. The drawer was locked but it was no match for Viktor's skillset as he picked it quite easily exposing the perfect tool - a dagger! The small blade was extraordinarily shiny and extremely sharp. While unable to comprehend it at the time, the knife almost seemed to compel Viktor to use it.

Carefully, he climbed onto the desk trying his best not to knock anything over. He reached up and jammed the tip into the opening in the ceiling and pushed with all his might until the secret hatch popped open. However with all the excitement and the momentum of his follow-through, the dagger slipped; leaving a three-inch cut across his cheek. The pain was searing but Viktor put the knife in his pocket and reached in to grab the contents in the ceiling - there was a box! It didn't look exactly like the chest Rubella had described; but 'finders keepers' he thought to himself.

He closed the hatch and hopped off the desk - the perfect crime he thought. Viktor made his way back to the window and rejoiced as he could still hear the old man's rhythmic heavy breathing.

Before he left however, he felt an overwhelming sense of wickedness consume him and completely ignored the fact he didn't have what Rubella had sent him for. He needed to know what he had stolen.

Viktor slowly opened the box and was immediately filled with wonder as a bright blue light burst through; his eyes fixated on his prize. He knew this was worth more than any payment from Rubella.

He thought to himself, 'she would never know.' Ignoring his conscience, Viktor seemed to convince himself. 'I'll tell her I couldn't find the chest, no harm done.'

Viktor promptly escaped out the window and ran back to his house feeling like a crowned champion. He was too preoccupied with greed and deception to recognize the new dark path that lay ahead.

A few weeks had passed since Viktor's luck had seemed to change, but he was unaware that an unexpected visitor would be surprising his lovely wife at home. Lara had fair skin, beautiful hair and despite her tiny facial features, she could be quite pretty.

She was a good woman and a supportive housewife who placed a lot of faith in her man. Lara was well aware of her partner's crooked trade, but her hopes of his reform were also clouded by her enduring love.

Her typical afternoon, while Viktor was out pilfering, was often spent drinking tea in her kitchen while sitting quietly in her favourite rocking chair. Lara was then obviously quite startled when she heard a knock at her quaint cottage door.

An old lady covered in a dark veil stood before her with a beautiful basket of food.

"Hello sweet thing." Looking down at Lara's large belly, "I see you're with child. What a blessing. I've brought you a lovely gift."

Lara smiled gratefully at the old lady while rubbing her enlarged baby bump. "Oh yes, my little one is almost due. Thank you so much. Please come in."

When Lara took the dish from the old lady and headed to the kitchen, the disguised visitor secretly pulled a hex bag from her purse and tucked it behind a chair. It seemed Viktor's apparent failure to deliver the chest did indeed have a penalty; Rubella was not forgiving.

Thinking her little trick went unnoticed, she was startled when she saw a young boy sitting in the corner staring at her. The child was no more than three years old, but his wholesome gaze was far from innocent. As Rubella stared into the icy blue eyes of the toddler, she felt her mind being infiltrated. Having strong powers of her own, she was able to resist, but could easily sense that the young boy was incredibly gifted.

"Extraordinary!" She said out loud.

Lara returned to witness the exchange and quickly intervened. "Grayson! Leave this old woman alone. I'm so sorry madam, he's my nephew and we're taking care of him for a little while. I know he can be a bother sometimes, but don't worry."

"Oh nonsense, children are precious."

They both watched as Grayson returned to play with some toys. He giggled as he levitated a ball and made it rotate around his head.

Rubella gasped, "Oh he's magnificent." She could see Lara was uncomfortable with the child's display of magic in front of a stranger. "Don't worry my dear, I won't say a thing."

Lara was at ease and then quickly changed the subject. She held up a piece of paper that had been embedded in the food basket. "What's this she asked? Is this Latin? *'vor dem bittet mor..'*"

The old lady interrupted her, "Oh don't read that now. It's a phrase that will kindle a spark within you; often said right before a meal. So wait until your husband is home and you can both enjoy the feast I prepared."

The women exchanged smiles and regards and as they parted ways, Lara suddenly felt an unexplained chill in the air. Queen Rubella walked away with a vicious grin and devious laugh. She looked back at the wholesome cottage and took delight in the fact that she had just unleased hell onto that family.

Chapter 10

As the Princess was still distraught over her near-death experience, she didn't even realize that her old nemesis was standing next right to her. Ambrosia took out her frustrations on the creature; screaming belligerently at its corpse and kicking it a few times to make sure it was fully dead.

Her overreactions caught the Evil Wizard by surprise; although Midnight was even more shocked when the old man reached down to help her up.

Midnight hesitantly said, "Thank you?"

As the two old enemies locked eyes, she was starting to consider that maybe making friends in the Badlands wasn't such a bad idea. She pointed to his kill, "A s7/8pear? That's not like you."

The Evil Wizard spoke softly but ominously in his deep throaty voice. "No magic can be used in this cave. It's quite dangerous for us."

Looking over at the agitated Princess, he continued. "What's with her? She seems…different."

Ambrosia had just begun to calm down when the sound of the Evil Wizard's voice triggered old memories and she turned to face him.

"Princess Ambrosia!" He said, smirking.

"Evil Wizard!" She replied with a stone-cold stare.

With such an intense history between the two foes, one could practically taste the animosity in the air.

Frankie broke the awkward silence. "Hey wizard, we need your help! Something is terribly wrong with the Princess."

The Evil Wizard hadn't even noticed Frankie, but was surprisingly cordial towards the firefly considering he had helped Ambrosia numerous times in their battles.

The old man looked up and down at the Princess. She was covered in mud and there were still remnants of animal guts splattered across her rainbow dress.

"You must be desperate. You've come all this way to this horrific place. Please tell me you have a way for us to get home?"

The shrewd look between Midnight, Frankie and Ambrosia was enough for the Princess to fraudulently offer the wizard a way back home in exchange for helping her find a cure.

"I agree to your terms, anything to get out of here. Now we must leave this cave immediately; there are many more dangerous creatures in this area. Follow me." At this point they had no choice but to form an alliance with the Evil Wizard but understandably continued to be cautious.

Of the three travellers, Frankie had the kindest heart; thus making it difficult to align himself with the underhanded plan of double-crossing the Evil Wizard. To accommodate his guilty conscience, he decided to strike up a conversation with the old man as they found an interim place to rest.

"Um, how did you even survive here?" The Evil Wizard looked at Frankie with some admiration and winked at him.

"Oh my old friend, a wizard never reveals his tricks. But I've had many close calls these past few months. I've been attacked, bitten, beaten, stabbed, skewered and practically killed several times."

The old man continued with his tales of horror, but one part of the story reverberated in Frankie's ears, almost confusing him; something he could not get past.

"Hey, what do you mean by 'old friend'?"

But before the wizard could answer, the Princess piped up with intense anger. "Just stop!"

She began screaming right into the wizard's face. "You came to MY kingdom and you tried to destroy ME! You got exactly what you deserved - because you're evil!"

The old man snapped back. "No! It is YOU who come from evil, not me!"

The words seemed to echo throughout the Badlands as the wizard's surprising revelation shook them to their core. He could see in their puzzled faces that he needed to explain further.

He sighed. "Ambrosia, the truth is your parents were dark, malicious sorcerers who conquered the kingdom and claimed the throne for themselves."

The Princess shook her head in disbelief.

He grabbed her close. "Let me see your eyes! Oh yes, I see the Darkness has started to consume you."

Midnight mumbled, "The Darkness?" It was almost as if she'd had heard of it before, possibly from her mother.

The Wizard continued his narrative. "The Darkness is an unspeakable evil and an unstoppable force. It is a malevolent entity of sin and wickedness that can blacken the whitest of lights and the purest of hearts. It's an ancient relic from the original wizards and witches that simply cannot and will not be stopped.

"I've had several run-ins with this sinister spirit; even been consumed by it. Its raw dark power is unmatched and unlimited. There are two parts to the Darkness, attaching itself to objects where it begins to slowly corrupt its owner's soul,

"Tracking the path of the Darkness has been difficult over the years. But right before you were born Ambrosia, your thieving father stole among other things, my cursed dagger. Your mother was also possessed by the dark entity, but I was never able to place when and where that old witch Rubella transferred the curse over to her.

"Ambrosia, you were born innocent but unknowingly grew up surrounded by pure evil. I felt somewhat responsible for the destruction of the kingdom, so I tried to overthrow your parents. I was almost completely outmatched by their dark sorcery and power, but I was able to defeat them by creating a magical vortex that swallowed them in.

"Your parents were wicked but still quite cunning, and just before they disappeared they transferred the Darkness to nearby objects. Viktor, your father was nearest to me at the time, and so my magic wand became its newest host; sending me on a corrupt path where I notoriously became - an evil wizard.

"I was never able to determine what your mother did with her inner demon. With you starting to harness your magical abilities, I knew I had to rid you of any memories. I sent you through an amnesia-type portal hoping and praying you'd come clean on the other side."

Midnight and Frankie were glued to the wizard's story and became more enthralled with every twist and turn. As the wizard completed his history lesson, he turned his focus to the Princess. However, she was stuck in a trance-like state; possibly suffering from shock. Maybe her repressed memories had finally started to return.

"Now that brings us to you, Princess. You must have something that the Darkness has possessed.

Pointing to Ambrosia's bear, "What is that?"

The Princess was very protective of her new friend and her attitude changed immediately.

"No, this is Rana, my bear. I found her with some other junk in an underground bunker near my castle. Look at her, she is not the Darkness. This is ridiculous!"

The Wizard cocked an eyebrow when she mentioned the bunker, but took a good look at the raggedy animal; almost losing himself in its soulless black pearly eyes. He then grabbed the collar to get a closer look at the chipped pendant which did indeed say 'Rana'.

The Wizard quickly dropped the bear like a hot potato and almost turned white with fear. The panic in his eyes was frightening; they had never seen him so terrified.

"That is not *Rana*! There are two letters missing! It is the true name of evil incarnate!"

The Princess began to mumble something under her breath.

He immediately shivered with fright, recalling an old memory at the quarry when he and his young witch friend had first discovered and released the Darkness.

Rubella had been overcome with the evil spirit and had whispered the dark entity's name in his ear. The sounds of her raspy voice made him numb with fear and he was left with a lifetime of nightmares from this inescapable horrific feeling.

The Princess turned to him with a demonic and twisted face and in a deep throaty voice that was not her own, she whispered into his ear '*MO-RANA*'.

The wizard felt the return of the terrorized chill vibrate through his body and mind. Ambrosia raised the bear and accepted the evil abomination to overtake her as black smoke exited the eyes of her stuffed toy and seemed to flow into her soul.

Both Frankie and Midnight screamed in horror as their friend succumbed to evil and they watched Princess Ambrosia go into the darkness.

The transformation in her face was quick as her sunken eyes blackened and her skin tone began to fade to a pale white.

The Dark Princess felt a massive surge of power within her and she immediately altered her glorious rainbow outfit into that of something far more insidious.

Princess Ambrosia dressed herself all in black. She had a thick-black cloak with a thick-black robe. She gave herself long black socks and the blackest of shoes. Her dark crooked smile was then complemented by her jet-black lipstick.

Being in the presence of pure evil was absolutely frightening and the sudden chill in the air was numbing.

She suddenly cackled loudly like a crazed maniacal witch and then ran off into the Badlands leaving her stunned companions speechless.

Chapter 11

Frankie was the first to speak. "What just happened to the Princess?" His tone was that of desperation but quickly turned to impatience when the wizard did not immediately reply.

Desperate for answers, he began to fly up into the old man's face, but Midnight jumped in front and began to calm the firefly down. She could see the wizard was visibly shaken and gently rested her hand on his shoulder giving him the friendly reassurance he needed.

Finally he gathered his composure. "Well it seems that the Princess herself has been invaded by the Darkness. It's taken over her body and soul and it will stop at nothing to seek out and destroy us."

Midnight and Frankie looked at each other with gloom and despair. Frankie was beside himself, almost inconsolable from the news that his best friend was now a demonic entity hell-bent on killing them.

Midnight was more practical during these emotional times and tried to keep the team focused on the mission.

"Okay, so what do we do? How do we stop her?"

Frankie blurted out, "We're not killing her, Evil Wizard. So don't even think about it!"

The old wizard cocked his head at Frankie.

"Okay, enough of this Evil Wizard nonsense! I am not evil anymore and I am no longer under the influence of the Darkness. Please, please, my name is Astarroth."

Midnight opened her mouth and wanted to speak but the words were slow to form. "You know, I think I've heard of you. My mother talked about you a lot. Although it was more screaming than talking."

"Oh yes, Rubella and I go back a long time. She and I were the ones to originally awaken the Darkness. What fools we were! I should have known better, and I'm still paying the price. Anyways, we have much bigger issues now!"

Midnight and Frankie really could not handle any more bad news.

"It's now going to try and find the other half of the Darkness."

"The other half is here? In the Badlands?"

Astarroth began pacing, almost stalling to tell them the answer. "Yes. If you recall, back when I was opening the Great Seal to this wretched place, the Princess destroyed my wand. The other part of the Darkness that had buried itself in there was then released into the closest object at the time."

"The Ring!" shouted Frankie, to which the old man firmly nodded.

"If she consumes the other half, she will become the full embodiment of the Darkness, the ultimate vessel of absolute evil."

He paused for a moment and then put his hand to his mouth. "She'll also have the magical power of the ring! Oh dear what have I done? She will be unstoppable! Come, the Ring is not far from here."

Midnight perked up. "Wait, you've known this whole time that the Ring is here? And you could have used it to escape this place?"

There was no hiding the obvious remorse in Astarroth's sullen face, living his entire life full of regret from having opened that chest. He truly believed it was his responsibility to bear, and the weight of the kingdom was on his shoulders.

"Yes, with my knowledge and power of the Ring, I likely could have escaped. But to what end? To be consumed by wickedness? To return as the Evil Wizard? NO, never again! The Darkness feeds on your emotions and your weaknesses, making you feel glorious and invincible. I refuse to be tempted a second time. I'm tired of hurting those I swore to protect."

Frankie and Midnight admired the wizard's courage and convictions. His inspiring speech gave them hope and instilled new trust in possibly their most powerful ally.

The treasured moment of optimism was suddenly short-lived with the incoming sounds of mutants screeching all around them. While the Badlands was notorious for its sadistic dangers and menacing wildlife, many who had perished there had already succumbed to the madness inflicted by its haunting noises.

Frankie always felt vulnerable because of his delicate body and lack of magic. So unsurprisingly he was especially susceptible to the constant fear of the tormenting growls and roars that reverberated in this emptiness. The howling trees echoing in the wasteland only further added to his panic and hysteria.

The thunderous grumbling of monsters seemed to be getting louder and closer, but nobody in the group could pinpoint their location.

"How many are there?" Frankie fearfully asked.

"Where are they?" His anxiety heightened further with the addition of a disturbing laugh seemingly pulsing from all directions.

It was the Princess!

Astarroth reminded them, "Be alert! Those creatures you hear - she's controlling them. We need to be ready to fight! Frankie, you'd better hide."

Astarroth barely finished his warning when he was suddenly struck from behind by a giant ogre. These types of beasts were common in the Badlands, not known for their intelligence but always formidable in a fight.

This hulky giant was about twelve feet tall; his body protected by its dense greyish-brown skin that was covered in short prickly fur. This particular one had a lazy eye as well as long sharp horns on each shoulder. An ogre's most powerful weapon was their strength as they often enjoyed ripping their prey's limbs off with ease.

Midnight gasped as the wizard was knocked down hard into the greasy mud. She wanted to help, but was startled by two enormous lizards charging towards her with malice. They were menacing reptiles with long jagged tails and insanely-sharp claws. Their blackened eyes and scaly skin only added to their threatening appearance.

Luckily for Midnight, the orange-haired witch had great reflexes. She touched her powerful emerald allowing her to levitate above her enemy's clutches.

She looked down upon the two agitated lizards with a touch of overconfidence and was definitely unprepared for a counter-attack. Their revenge was swift as the female produced two large spanning wings and flew up towards the sorceress with incredible speed. Midnight tried to avoid its reach but it carved her like a scalpel with a clean cut across her arm about three inches long.

She screamed in pain and had no choice but to return to the surface where the male was still lurking and hungry. Midnight ran off to heal and hide but also readying herself for their next attack.

Astarroth finally stood up to face his grisly opponent who towered over him.

The ogre was eager to land a crushing blow which would certainly have killed the old man. But the behemoth's swings and punches could not strike the magical wizard as he constantly teleported himself at will.

Astarroth's elegance and skill had overmatched the ogre's brute force; the mutant beast left visibly frustrated and enraged.

The wizard looked off into the darkened distance to see fireballs being launched in the air at a shrieking flying lizard. The old man raced towards the blazing battlefield to help out Midnight while the giant stubborn oaf followed.

The witch's powers were quite strong and effective, but they were not unlimited. She soon ran out of ammunition and with the female returning to the ground, her demise seemed inevitable.

Both monsters had her cornered and they could practically smell her exposed blood as they moved in for the kill. Midnight took a deep breath and closed her eyes, preparing to join her sisters in the afterlife.

Suddenly one of the creatures made a horrendous noise and flopped over, unable to move. Midnight opened her eyes to see the wizard standing over the fallen beast; his hand on her belly soothing her to sleep.

Midnight was amazed. "That was incredible! How did you do that?"

Astarroth laughed. "Oh Midnight, one day I'll teach you. But we still have one more and he is really angry!"

She then shouted, "Behind you!"

The ogre was still quite determined and charged hard at the old man like a battering ram. Astarroth turned around quickly and with a stern look on his face, raised his hand at the bullish beast with great confidence. The giant lug just froze in its tracks and could not move.

Again, Midnight was utterly impressed; she had never seen such magic before.

The other frenzied lizard attacked as well, thrashing its dangerous tail right at them. The quick-thinking wizard snapped his fingers and both he and Midnight vanished causing a chain reaction of the lizard striking the ogre.

They reappeared to find themselves witnessing an epic battle between two of the Badlands' fiercest creatures. Not wanting to stick around, Midnight and Astarroth walked away with pride listening to the sounds of the monsters' primal cries.

Just up the path from them was a large black swamp, and as Astarroth began to lean against a tree to catch his breath, he felt the branches move.

He called out, "Midnight get out of here! Go find Frankie."

She looked on in horror as the old man quickly became entangled in the tree's long vines squeezing him tight against its trunk.

Before she could even help him, she was interrupted by the Princess. "Do you mean this Frankie?"

Ambrosia gracefully floated in from the night sky with Frankie the Firefly firmly in her grasp. They had almost forgotten about the Princess and how dangerous she would be. It had all happened so fast before but now they were able to fully assess their dire situation. They looked into her soulless eyes and saw nothing but emptiness and death.

Her voice was raspy, abhorrent and downright frightening. "Well well well, what do we have here? I've missed you Astarroth."

The wizard had faced off against the Darkness in the past, and as powerful as he was, its evil and malevolent existence always instilled fear in him. Still unable to move from the tight animated branches keeping him prisoner, he called out. "Let Frankie go! This is between you and me."

Ambrosia looked at him up and down with a devilish smile. "Oh but first you'll do something for me."

The Princess quickly turned towards a familiar face. "Won't you Midnight?"

Midnight was petrified and in utter shock at the grotesque appearance of her good friend.

"I just need you to retrieve the Ring from that swamp, and he's all yours."

The Wizard immediately shouted. "No Midnight, you mustn't!"

At first the Princess chuckled like a little girl, but she quickly changed her tune to that of a crazed lunatic. Her eyes wide open, her face full of hatred; she began to pull on Frankie's wings!

"If you don't get in that swamp and bring me my Ring, I'm going to rip his tiny little wings right off!"

Midnight had never seen so much rage and hostility. She knew Ambrosia was not bluffing. "Okay okay, I'll go, just don't hurt him."

Frankie on the other hand was beyond terrified, shaking and quivering with fear. His mind raced with thoughts of suffering and pain; recalling the visions the Princess had in her dreams.

"Midnight," the old man called out. "That is no ordinary water you'll be going in. It's full of enchanted black tar that will boil you alive if you're not careful."

The Princess stretched Frankie a bit more as his screams forced Midnight to make her descent into the tar swamp. As Midnight walked in, she could feel the thickness of the tar coating her legs. Steam started to rise from the depths of the swamp as large bubbles began to form on the surface. She was up to her waist when the temperature rose swiftly causing her to cry out in pain. Frankie and Astarroth closed their eyes, they simply could not watch the torture and pain Midnight was about to endure.

Up to her neck in the boiling swamp, heavy steam rose from the depths as the amount of tar bubbles rapidly increased. As tears flowed down her face, they quickly evaporated from the intense heat. They could all see Midnight's cheeks blistering and burning; Frankie looked on in anguish. Her piercing cries were finally silenced as she submerged herself into the death trap. The entire ordeal amused the Princess as she seemed to feast on their suffering.

The anticipation was excruciating for her friends, not knowing if Midnight would even return. Finally her head emerged from the scorching tar, her gaping mouth yearning for oxygen. She slowly was able to reach the shore, but the torment and pain she endured was unbearable.

Her body was covered in blisters and boils, the skin on her face almost completely melted; she was barely recognizable. She knelt down on the ground coughing and writhing in pain. She slowly was able to reach up to her necklace and through the thick black tar, healed herself through the power of her shimmering emerald.

The Princess was impressed and released Frankie and started clapping. "Wonderful!"

Frankie was quite traumatized but he was still in one piece. He was also unbelievably grateful his friend Midnight was okay.

"So my dear, did you get it?"

Midnight was non-responsive, she was still on her knees refusing to get up or reveal if she had indeed retrieved the Ring.

Ambrosia was extremely impatient and the demon inside her suddenly snapped. The Princess grabbed Midnight by the neck and lifted her high up; the Darkness had made her strong and full of madness.

"Give me the Ring," she demanded as she squeezed her hand tighter around her friend's neck. Midnight shook her head defiantly.

Astarroth pleaded, "Don't do this Ambrosia. You can fight it!" The Princess stopped for a moment, loosening her grip a bit as Midnight caught a few quick gasps. "No old timer, your sweet Ambrosia is gone! There is only Morana!"

With one last look into Midnight's surrendering eyes, the Dark Princess unleashed her menacing power and rage. She squeezed excessively hard as Midnight's life began to wither away. Her beautiful blue eyes began to shrivel and roll up into the back of her head; her beautiful skin turned to a soft grey. Finally her bright emerald green necklace, the beacon of her power, dimmed and flickered out.

Then her life ultimately faded away.

Frankie screamed and cried in agony as he watched his friend suffocate to death with such malice and force. The Wizard could not bear to watch or witness the destruction he had caused. It was too painful.

Ambrosia held the deceased witch's lifeless body until she went limp. Midnight finally released her clenched fist dropping the Ring right into the hand of the Dark Princess.

Chapter 12

It was not too long ago that peace and nobility were commonplace in the kingdom. The King and Queen, proudly alongside their son, had ruled triumphantly with little conflict for many years.

The use of sorcery was not prohibited, with only a select few possessing such power, often performing secretly. The leading monarchy didn't possess any magic themselves, but had a strong family history of leadership, generosity and a reputation that only strengthened their rule.

The Prince was an honourable and caring young teenager revered in the lands as the next generation's great ruler. With flowing auburn hair, the Prince was tall for his age, always well-dressed and was known for his kind heart.

Growing up, he had spent most days within the castle walls as his overprotective parents forbade him to associate himself with the townsfolk. He couldn't develop any real friendships except for the occasional children whose rich aristocratic parents visited His or Her Majesty.

So it was no surprise that the young Prince had befriended a powerful old wizard who often worked at the castle as the Royal Aide and Protector.

Since the young royal's birth, Astarroth had nothing but adoration and affection for the Prince as he watched him mature into a young man. The great wizard would often surprise him with small gifts and often mystify his little companion with wonders of magic. Nothing gave Astarroth more pleasure than seeing the young boy's face light up with simple acts of illusions and enchantments.

One evening, the old man was working in his study mixing potions and developing new spells. He was then interrupted by the familiar sounds of the young Prince knocking at his door.

"Yes yes, come in my boy," he shouted out.

The Prince inquired, "Astarroth, how did you know it was me?"

With a charming wink Astarroth replied, "Oh a wizard never reveals his tricks. What can I do for you?"

"Well I've got to attend one of my father's fancy dinners and help entertain his new guests. But I thought maybe you'd show me a new trick before I'm bored to death down there."

"Oh right, the dinner party. I hear they have a daughter, almost your age?"

The young Prince lit up with excitement at first, and then bit his bottom lip as nerves began to set in quickly.

"Oh nonsense," Astarroth smirked. "You don't have to marry the girl. Just be yourself. There's nothing to be afraid of."

To calm the Prince, the grand wizard snapped his fingers and levitated the cup of wine on his desk. Astarroth then guided it slowly across the room as the young adolescent watched in wonder as it landed comfortably in his own hands. "One small sip for good luck; I won't tell the Queen."

The boy's grin widened as he carefully sipped the forbidden drink; the warm red liquid soothing his fears instantly. Sensing the Prince's eager thirst, Astarroth magically commanded the cup back, whipping it out of the boy's firm grip like a snapped elastic band.

The quick action startled and embarrassed the boy, but his first taste of wine had already started to work its wonders.

"Thanks Astarroth," the Prince said with such gratitude and elation. The proud wizard said nothing, but returned back a gleaming smile.

With a new sense of courage and swagger, the young man headed to dinner, ready to do his duty and greet his parents' guests. They were already seated at the long dinner table when he had arrived, the adults talking and laughing. He immediately noticed the young quiet girl sitting alone, avoiding the conversation. Her face was full of innocence and she had beautiful wavy light brown hair and a stunning dress - she was pretty.

The Prince, not having developed many friendships in his youth, especially with those of the opposite sex, was immediately smitten with the daughter. She was the first to speak; her soft voice only furthered his attraction.

"Hi, my name is Ambrosia. You of course must be the Prince."

He replied. "Yes, but you can call me Frankie."

The two exchanged awkward smiles and continued to stumble through the customary small-talk throughout dinner. Frankie found it difficult at times to find similar interests to Ambrosia as he mostly led a sheltered life.

His hobbies were often limited to the castle and so they didn't have comparable life experiences.

Ambrosia had always been enamoured with the idea of royalty and all the riches and power that came with it. Ever since she was a little girl she dreamt of visiting the castle. All those times in front of the mirror pretending to be a Princess - and here she was having dinner with Prince Frankie!

"What's it like being the Prince? How many servants do you have? It must be so exciting!"

Her enthusiasm was bordering on obnoxious, but the Prince did not want to disappoint his dinner date.

Rather than disheartening Ambrosia, he confirmed her theories about the flashy facade of royalty lifestyle.

Frankie felt hollow inside as he really wanted to ask her about the hustle and bustle of the town square, or the fun activities that occur in the village. Specifically, the types of games they played, the events they had; anything that was better than the posh prison he was born into.

He tried to find common ground to work in some questioning when he noticed a sparkling blue wonder on her hand. "That's a really beautiful ring you have on."

She looked over with enthusiasm. "Yes! My dad gave it to me for my birthday. It's sooo nice. It's made out of sapphire."

She then whispered, "Hey, you want to see a cool trick?"

She subtly raised her finger and she began to manipulate a fork on the table, quivering it back and forth. Frankie was awestruck. "You can do magic?"

Ambrosia shhed him, but continued to boast. "Yes, my family is quite gifted. I'm starting to get good, although my cousin is amazing – but I'm not supposed to talk about him."

The Prince was hooked on her every word. "What other tricks can you do?"

Her ego began to take over. "Well I can move small objects. But what I'm really good at is producing rainbow light or fire from my fingers. I'm still practising. Can you do any magic Frankie?"

The way Ambrosia asked him was devastating for Frankie, as he looked into her hopeful eyes and could not bear the thought of disappointing her. He couldn't lie or fake his way through that question, but he brilliantly thought of an angle to pique her interest further.

"No. But if you want to see some awesome magic, I know the greatest wizard in the kingdom. Maybe he can show us some tricks?"

Ambrosia was of course interested, having almost become obsessed ever since she learned of her skills and magical lineage.

The two teens excused themselves and Frankie took Ambrosia by the hand and they snuck upstairs to go visit the wizard's study. The Prince knocked on the door hoping to introduce a fellow conjurer to his old friend, but Astarroth did not answer.

With a newly acquired sense of fearlessness and bravado, Frankie opened the door and let himself and Ambrosia in. She looked around with immense fascination as the old wizard had several books, potions and charmed items in and around his desk.

She immediately began to look and touch anything she could get her hands on.

Frankie began to get a bit nervous. "Okay just be careful in here, I don't know what everything does. I don't want us to get hurt or get in trouble."

Ambrosia was too excited to heed any advice from Frankie and continued to peruse the wizard's various books with endless curiosity. It was typical of young sorcerers to be overconfident with their powers, often developing a dangerous sense of invincibility with no worry of consequences. Even though Ambrosia had just begun to understand her powers and limits, she's had a history of getting into trouble.

Her parents had to invest in a pair of anti-charmed gold bracelets; a marvellous device for restricting magic, and an excellent parenting tool for controlling little witches and wizards who misbehaved. The idea was genius – place one around the child's wrist and the magic was stifled - to unlock, simply put the other matching pair on the opposite wrist.

She motioned to Frankie to keep a look-out, and when his head was turned, she swiped a small purple vial from Astarroth's desk and slipped it into her handbag.

The Prince was not the sneaky type, so he finally asserted himself and demanded that Ambrosia leave. Much to his surprise and relief, she obeyed almost immediately and quickly left the wizard's den. However, Frankie was unaware that Ambrosia only did so because of her nifty little crime. She had hoped to experiment with this fancy magic when she got home.

The two youths explored the castle some more until they found themselves alone in the Great Hall. The largest room in the castle had large glass windows and a vast empty space that turned most noises into thundering echoes.

"This place is huge," she said looking around in awe. "Oh oh this is the perfect spot to show you some magic. Watch this."

She didn't even wait for him to respond, she raised her arm hoping to put on a massive fireworks display. However all she could muster was a few tiny white sparks from the tip of her finger. Frankie was impressed and continued to encourage Ambrosia but she was embarrassed and frustrated; so she tried again repeatedly.

Finally on the fourth attempt, the white sparks erupted into a glowing white light that eventually alternated into the colours of the rainbow. She was able to control the light for only a few seconds before it fizzled out; Frankie was amazed as he continued to cheer her on.

Ambrosia saw the big look of wonder and approval on the Prince's face; she wanted to impress him more - maybe one day she'd be his bride and become the Princess.

She took the stolen potion from her small purse and smashed it to the ground in front of them. A little bit of the liquid landed on Frankie's polished white shoes. He barely noticed as he waited to see the outcome of this next trick.

Suddenly, the glass windows surrounding the Great Hall shattered everywhere as if there was an explosion. Purple smoke began to circulate in the air, but it seemed to dissipate quickly with no effect.

Frankie called out, "What was that supposed to do?" Ambrosia turned to him with a strange look noticing his cracked voice. Frankie noticed it too.

"What's wrong with my voice?" The more he spoke, the higher the pitch it became; he covered his mouth in embarrassment.

The King and Queen, along with Astarroth and Ambrosia's parents, had heard the detonation of the glass and had just walked in on them.

Suddenly Frankie's legs and arms began to shrink as fear and shock took over his innocent young face.

"What's happening to me?"

His mother the Queen screamed, "My beautiful Prince!"

As Ambrosia watched in horror, Frankie began to sprout wings from his back, piercing his skin and ripping his now bloody clothes.

It was all unfolding so fast, even the wizard stood there shaking not sure of what had happened or how to stop it.

Frankie continued to shrink, his bones breaking, his face and eyes shrivelling up and turning black - it was absolutely horrific to watch. Ambrosia screamed in terror as her charming Prince was being mutilated before her eyes; morphing into some kind of insect. His tiny tummy began to glow and the agonizing transformation was complete - he had become a firefly.

The Queen was in shock and in tears, while the King's rage was absolute and he demanded Ambrosia's execution. Sensing his family's imminent danger, Viktor pulled out his dagger and stabbed the King in the back, paralyzing him. Astarroth was too slow to react, and was knocked down by Lara who violently used a spell to launch him across the room.

Frankie flew clumsily to Astarroth and pleaded for help, his high-pitched voice quite apparent now. The wizard was in great physical pain and also devastated with grief as he looked up at his young deformed Prince.

He vowed, "I promise Frankie, I'll fix this!"

The former Prince would be in danger as a last remaining witness, so Astarroth waved his hand around the little firefly and applied a simple memory-blocking spell to keep him safe. Then before Viktor or Lara could inflict any more damage, he made himself and Frankie disappear.

The defenseless, crying Queen stood at the fallen body of her husband, praying and begging for mercy. She looked up and saw young Ambrosia staring back at her. The young girl's eyes were swollen, her face still flushed from the trauma. She held Frankie's golden crown in her hands and looked down at the overthrown leaders.

Even at Ambrosia's young age, she knew the deadly fate that would befall the King and Queen. She also recognized that a big change was coming and that magic would soon rule the kingdom.

But more importantly, her regret and mourning began to fade with the sudden realization that she may actually become the Princess.

Chapter 13

The newly crowned Queen of Darkness bit her lip with excitement as she placed the all-powerful Ring on her finger. She felt a surge of power as she began to utter the ancient words to summon the other half of the Darkness.

As her eyes fully blackened, dark purplish veins began to develop on her arms and legs. Electricity seemed to crackle and sizzle around her skin, continuously burning and healing as it flowed. Her rich ebony hair stood out against her soulless pale white face. The once delicate and beautiful Princess Ambrosia had now become menacing and grotesque. She had fully transformed into Morana - the true embodiment of the Darkness.

She focused her attention on Astarroth, as the tree's thorny vines continued to imprison him by squeezing him tight. Ambrosia laughed like an evil demented lunatic as she approached the suffering wizard.

"Well well well." She gently poked him on his nose; the touch of pure evil burned his skin.

"After thousands of years, I'm finally free! And I just love this new body, she's a perfect host. I'm going to have so much fun! Now, what should I do with you my old friend? I would love nothing more than to rip your soul from your worthless body and snap your neck like a twig. But you know what? I think you and this place deserve each other."

Astarroth could barely look at the Dark Princess, her crackling body and malevolent soul disgusted him. All he could see was the dark entity; there was nothing left of the girl he once knew. As she continued to mock and taunt him, the sounds of approaching creatures from all directions seemed to be headed his way.

"You hear that? They're coming! I'd love to stay and watch them devour you, but I have a kingdom to burn down and a world to conquer. You understand, right?"

She quickly pivoted away like lightning to where Frankie was hiding.

"Hey firefly, don't worry. I've got plans for you too. You're coming with me. I could use a good obedient slave!"

Frankie had still not recovered from the shock of Midnight's death, and was now being forced to be a servant for the devil. He grudgingly followed the Darkness but almost wished he had been compelled to stay in the Badlands with the wizard.

As he flew away, he took one last look at Astarroth and the two shared a sad lasting moment of defeat. The impending roars and growls were almost upon them and he could not bear to watch the old man's demise.

Ambrosia zapped Frankie and herself back to the Portal doorway as they headed back to their world. She sensed the firefly was hesitant. "Go on little Prince, get in there! Don't worry, when we get back to the castle, you'll learn how to obey through suffering and pain!"

While the Darkness knew all of their secrets, the comment about the Prince didn't resonate with Frankie. He was far too depressed and distracted from the recent tragic events to even notice.

Frankie complied and proceeded to fly right into the white glowing orb; but he was unsuccessful at breaking through.

Frustrated by his lack of success, Morana grabbed him by his wings and dragged him into the interdimensional gateway. The Dark Princess could also not penetrate the barrier and she lashed out in a frenzy of madness.

She blasted it with an assortment of lightning bolts and energy pulses. She threw every magical charm she had, but all her evil spells and dark tricks bounced off. Watching the irate Darkness repeatedly fail put a much needed smile on Frankie's face; especially since he knew why.

"Hey Ambrosia," he called out. She looked upon him with immense hatred. "If you remember, we need three to get through - it's an Absolute Portal!"

The Princess was quite vexed as she paced back and forth grunting and fuming with rage.

Suddenly she stopped and had an almost miraculous look on her face as if she had discovered gold. Ambrosia raised her hand brandishing the Ring and aimed it at the pulsing white light. Frankie stopped smiling.

The shimmering blue light of the Ring shot out and covered the gateway shaking it to its core. Gritting her teeth, Ambrosia clenched her fist even harder letting out a demonic roar as she attempted to blast through. She motioned for Frankie to try again, but he complied with minimal effort.

Morana, however, was relentless in her pursuit. She magically thrust Frankie's tiny body against the sphere; his face pushing hard against the ball of light. She hoped the Ring could be strong enough to find a small crack in the gateway's armour; enough for Frankie to slip through. But even with all that power and force, Midnight's simple portal was protected by even the most powerful magic.

Frustrated and baffled, the Princess lowered the Ring and released Frankie from her clutches. She could see the little firefly was attempting to talk while catching his breath. "Yes slave, spit it out!"

Frankie knew that Ambrosia would hate his idea, but he revelled in the irony of it. "Well Morana," he continued to enjoy this satisfying moment of leverage over the Dark Princess. "If we go back and rescue the wizard, we can bring him back with us."

Ambrosia scowled at the smug firefly and she stomped off into the direction of Astarroth with a sarcastic hope that the hordes of savage monsters had yet to feast on him.

She arrived back at the swamp to find some hungry beasts in disarray. They charged at her, but the Evil Darkness simply flung them aside like they were trash. More importantly, there was no trace of the wizard anywhere and Midnight's body was also gone. Frankie was relieved he didn't see any blood or remains. Further, he was thrilled to know his magical friend had likely escaped - maybe there was still hope.

Ambrosia screamed like a banshee with great fury, shaking the entire Badlands like an earthquake. She looked around for the great wizard and called him out to fight. At first she didn't get a response, but then suddenly she was blindsided by a strong magical force, knocking her into the boiling tar swamp.

With her veiny skin bubbling and blistering, she slowly walked out with a fat grin on her face as if she was enjoying the pain.

She looked high and far for the wizard waiting to see what he had planned next for her. She chuckled and called out, "Is that the best you got? Are you gonna kill this poor girl? Is that your plan?"

Astarroth suddenly revealed himself from a distance, his lustrous white beard almost glistening. He never looked so magical and energized as he did then.

Frankie was proud.

He floated down towards the Dark Princess as they stared each other down as if readying for an epic battle.

"You've left me no choice, Morana. I will do what is necessary to stop you from destroying the kingdom."

The Darkness didn't hesitate. She stomped on the ground with a colossal force cracking the earth in Astarroth's direction. The quake spread quickly and erratically as the wizard fell through into the unknown depths below. Frankie gasped as he watched from a distance.

Ambrosia then firmly clapped her hands with a huge force, sending ripples into the Badlands as she commanded the grounds to swallow the old man in. The surface slammed shut with a thundering boom that echoed throughout the underworld.

As the dust and dirt began to settle, there was no word or movement from the wizard below. Frankie started to get anxious but was soon given a glimpse of hope when he heard faint rumbling down at the surface.

The sound was low, but some gravel and rocks began to tumble as the tremors began to increase. Soon there was a massive eruption from the underbelly of the Badlands as Astarroth launched himself up through the ground sending dirt and mud all over the Dark Princess.

While he did not look as gleaming as before, the old man arrogantly dusted himself off only having a few scratches. The great wizard then looked straight at Ambrosia. "Is that the best *you* got?"

Ambrosia growled like a rabid dog at him. She leaned back and threw an onslaught of fireballs and lightning bolts at Astarroth, with the old man using all of his strength to deflect them.

He struggled to stay on his feet as she continued to blast him with everything she had.

The Darkness was far more powerful than the wizard, and deep down inside he knew it. He could not continue going toe-to-toe with her; he knew she would ultimately kill him.

Finally a burst of fire made its way through Astarroth's shielded magic and set him ablaze. He fell to the ground screaming and writhing in pain. Luckily, the accomplished wizard used some quick-thinking magic to suffocate the flames. Unfortunately, it was not fast enough as much of his body had intense burns. Most severely, his back and legs were badly scarred, with parts of his robe fused to his blistery skin.

Frankie flew down to check on his friend. "Are you okay Astarroth? She's killing you!"

Princess Ambrosia strutted around them with an unpleasant cockiness, laughing and mocking their defeat. The old man grimaced in pain as it took all his energy to stand up. "I'm okay Frankie. But I'm not dead yet."

The Darkness glared down at Astarroth, "Oh but you will be soon."

Suddenly she let out a giant deafening roar that felt deep and menacing. The hefty sound seemed to vibrate quickly throughout the Badlands like a sonic boom. For a few moments afterwards, there was a complete and utter silence that greatly concerned the two remaining heroes.

The mystery surrounding the unknown spell or demonic wish the Princess had just casted was frightening.

But the silence quickly faded as faint screeches and growls from every direction seemed to build up. The earth began to shake as moving shadows in the distance became thicker as they approached the battleground.

The wizard stood and watched as all the unsavoury creatures and rabid beasts in the Badlands were headed their way. It only took a couple of minutes, but Morana stood before them having compiled her own army of horrific monsters raging behind her.

The sounds of their gnashing teeth, scraping claws and ghastly screams were more than enough reason for Frankie to fly back in hiding.

Astarroth looked at the angry swarm of giant barbarians and knew they were desperate to rip him apart. Morana was unforgiving in her attack and raised her arm commanding the frenzied mutants to attack the wizard.

Hundreds of deranged wild animals, the worst of the worst of the Badlands, barrelled down at Astarroth as he prepared himself for perhaps his final act.

He slowly knelt down on one knee and wiped a bit of blood in his hand and closed his eyes.

He called out loudly.

"nostrum varvatos ela pulvis"

His spell was quick as the blood from his hand erupted towards the violent horde, turning each and every creature into dust. One by one, their thick-skinned scales and razor-sharp claws withered and crumbled into a light black powder; and then it was silent once again.

Morana's eyes widened with shock and astonishment as her murderous, bloodthirsty army had been vanquished in a matter of seconds. However, the

Darkness loved witnessing power and was mildly impressed with the wizard.

"Well well, somebody has been reading my book it seems. I should have known you couldn't resist."

Astarroth could never fully ignore the dark magic contained in the book of his ancestors. He had secretly studied it for many years until Queen Rubella finally got her hands on it.

He had never actually used any of the ancient spells before and suddenly began to realize how much of a toll it took. The wizard felt uncomfortably woozy as the effects of the hallowed incantation seemed to penetrate his soul.

With the old man suffering and visibly wounded, the unstoppable Darkness insisted on inflicting more pain. Using the magical Ring, she lifted up her rival, tossed him in the air and then launched him several hundred feet against the rocky terrain. His momentum took him beyond a cliff and Astarroth fell hard to the ground below.

Frankie flew as fast as he could to check on the wizard. The old man's injuries were serious as he was covered in mud and blood and bruises all over. He looked up and saw a nearby cave and desperately tried to drag his crumpled body over there to take shelter.

As he inched towards the mouth of the cave, his torn and battered body dragging on the ground, he could hear the inevitable footsteps of the Darkness above. She hovered high above him with a victorious look on her face.

"You fought well Astarroth, but your time has come."

Morana lifted her hand producing a hot white ball of fire, readying herself for the final fatal blow. She reared back but was interrupted by a ghostly spirit - it was Midnight!

The Darkness was incensed with the vision of the young witch. "You! I already killed you!"

The unfazed dead witch smiled at Morana.

"Of anyone, you should know better that the only true way to get rid of a witch is to burn her body. I am going to enjoy haunting you."

Ambrosia extinguished her deadly weapon and grinned. "You know what I enjoyed? Killing you and watching your life fade away right in front of me. That is exactly how I'm going to finish the old man."

She flew right through Midnight's transparent spirit and landed near the decrepit wizard; who had pulled himself onto a pile of old animal bones.

She walked towards him as Frankie flew down to desperately try to convince her to stop.

"Morana. If you kill him, then we'll be stuck here forever!"

The evil entity did not care anymore; it was going to destroy the wizard and very much likely eliminate Frankie as well.

The wizard had managed to turn himself over and was now face-to-face with the Evil Princess!

She leaned over and prepared to crush him with a final deadly spell, but seemed unable to wield it. She tried several spells, even pointing the magical ring at the wounded wizard, but she still came up empty.

Just then, Astarroth grabbed one of the bones and firmly bashed Ambrosia with a strong blow to the head, knocking her out cold. "No magic in here Princess!"

Frankie was buzzing frantically, "You did it! But is she okay?"

Astarroth leaned over, touching Ambrosia's shoulder. "Oh yeah, she's alive. But she won't wake for a bit."

He pulled himself up with all of his remaining strength and hobbled towards the cave entrance dragging the Princess with him. He pulled the Ring off her finger and held it in hands. It had been a long time since he felt its power.

He then chanted the familiar phrase *"vor dem bittet morana seco vivia elos caza"* and thick black smoke withdrew from Ambrosia's ears and nose and emptied itself into the Ring.

Her haggard appearance slowly began to revert as warmth finally returned to her skin and the black in her irises diminished to its normal shimmering green.

Astarroth stared at the now dangerous sapphire and gazed at its wondrous light. He had only had a small taste of the Darkness when he was the Evil Wizard and remembered how good it felt to have so much power and invincibility.

The blackened entity of Morana was already beginning to darken the wizard's soul just by him being in close proximity to its malevolent spirit. It called to the wizard, the voices in his head suggesting he 'put on the ring', 'just once', 'it would feel so good'.

Even the sounds of Frankie screaming at him were being smothered by the power of the Darkness. The wizard was losing his sense of reality but the sight of Frankie made him remember a promise he made many years ago.

Astarroth finally resisted the demons and flung the Ring as hard as he could deep into the cave. He immediately felt the dark emotions that were preying on his conscience begin to disappear.

With his own powers returned, he began to heal himself and watch his blisters, scabs and bruises all fade away. He was still incredibly sore and weakened but thankfully no longer in pain.

He magically hoisted himself and Ambrosia up to the top of the cliff and stood over the cave knowing what he must do. Raising a clenched fist, he exploded the ceiling of the cave toppling piles of dense rock and dirt everywhere; sealing in the Ring and the Darkness forever.

Astarroth breathed a huge sigh of relief as he hoped to never come across true Evil again.

Frankie urged the wizard that it was time to leave and that he could show him the way out of this wretched place. On the way back, there were no monsters and no dangers; almost as if the Badlands were finally at peace.

Despite the unusual tranquility that surrounded them, they didn't want to hesitate when they reached the portal. However before they ventured back into their realm, they were interrupted by Midnight's familiar spirit.

Frankie flew over first and was broken-hearted to see his old friend. "I'm so sorry Midnight; I wish you could come home with us."

"It's okay my sweet firefly, this is still a happy ending. You are a good soul. Please take good care of the Princess."

The two shared a parting smile that left a tear in Frankie's eyes.

Astarroth headed over to talk to Midnight as Frankie flew off to give them some privacy. There was much magical history between the two and they both shared a beautiful moment of gratitude and respect.

They seemed to talk for quite a while with a lot of whispering; Frankie could not hear what they were discussing. Finally, Astarroth raised his hand in

Midnight's direction; her spirit began to fizzle until it disappeared.

"What was that about Astarroth?"

"Oh Frankie, Midnight and I had much to discuss. She's at peace now. Come on, let's get out of here."

The wizard picked up and carried Princess Ambrosia through the gateway with Frankie eagerly following alongside them. The three adventurers then passed through the blinding light of the Absolute Portal; their bodies filled with illumination. In an instant, they found themselves back in Midnight's run-down cabin; the doorway to a world of nightmares vanished behind them - they were finally home!

Chapter 14

They were immediately greeted by Jade who was distressed not to find her master. Astarroth could sense the little feline was getting restless, so he picked up the tabby to try and console her. He mumbled something under his breath, and the feisty kitten purred in his arms and then quickly dashed into a corner to hide.

Frankie was quite concerned about the Princess and wouldn't leave her side. She lay peacefully on Midnight's bed with a noticeable throbbing bruise on the side of her temple. He hoped Ambrosia would wake soon; he missed his friend dearly.

Astarroth came over and put a damp towel on her head, a thoughtfulness Frankie never thought was possible with the wizard. The old man looked down at the Princess, still sporting the Darkness' extreme gothic-like outfit, and proceeded to magically transform her back into her glorious rainbow ensemble.

Frankie leaned on the expertise and knowledge of the wizard. "She's going to be okay? Back to normal?"

"Oh yes. I mean she'll have a whopper of a headache for the next few days, but she'll be okay. Also, I can honestly say that being inhabited by the Darkness is no laughing matter. She will be consumed by guilt and regret, but trust me, she's quite strong-willed."

The wizard smiled as he recalled Princess Ambrosia's perseverance and determination in the past to defeat him. "She'll be just fine."

"You know Frankie; this might be a good time for us to have a chat. I'm guessing you have some questions about your past?"

This was a huge revelation for the firefly, and Frankie was bursting with excitement about the possibility of learning about his ancestry.

"As you know, you're quite special. I mean a talking firefly, and one so admirable and noble such as you, is quite unusual - even for us powerful sorcerers."

Frankie was hanging on his every word, but felt that

Astarroth was stalling a bit, almost as if he was embarrassed or felt shame.

"The truth is!" The wizard paused. "You were born human!"

The words rang through Frankie's ears and he became numb with euphoria after finally learning the truth. Frankie desperately needed more. "Well how did I get like this? What did I look like?"

"Well my young friend, you were quite a charming boy; and quite handsome."

While giving a sly look to the unconscious Princess, Astarroth wasn't quite ready to reveal the whole truth as some secrets are best kept hidden. He had to choose his words carefully.

"But unfortunately, you happened upon some very peculiar magic and you were transformed into your glowing little self."

Frankie was enthralled with the old man's tale and was hopeful the story would ultimately have a happy ending.

"So does that mean you can turn me back? You're a powerful wizard!"

Astarroth scratched his wavy white beard. "Well you see it's not that simple, unfortunately. I can't just snap my fingers and you become a person again. I need to replicate the magic precisely and get the ingredients right. One miscalculation and well, you could be killed; or worse, deformed."

This wasn't exactly what Frankie wanted to hear.

"But I promise you, after we get the Princess back to her castle, you and I will work together and find a cure."

The former Prince was full of hope and had great confidence in the wizard, especially after witnessing his strength and tenacity in the Badlands. He still had so many questions and couldn't wait to spend more time with Astarroth discovering the missing parts of his past.

But his attention quickly turned to the Princess as she finally began to stir. Feeling the bump on her head, she was woozy and a little disoriented, suffering from the effects of her massive headache. But as objects and people began to come into focus, she turned her attention with complete clarity to her white-haired nemesis.

Ambrosia's first instinct was to lash out, she had a lot of built up contempt for her Evil Wizard. But the recent memories of her wrongdoings in the Badlands quickly overpowered her emotions.

"Oh no! Midnight!" She covered her face in sheer panic and became distraught. The Princess broke down in tears as the realization of her actions started to settle in. "What have I done?"

Frankie wanted to be the one to comfort his friend, but as fate would be his misfortune, he lacked the physical body that he so desperately wanted.

Ambrosia became hysterical and erratic and so the old man sat beside the Princess and consoled her as best he could. The two had never shared any previous personal moments, but grief and sympathy can be a potent catalyst that binds any relationship.

She looked up at the old wizard and unloaded all of her mixed emotions. "Oh I almost killed you, I'm so sorry! That thing inside me made me do all those horrible things. I couldn't help myself."

Then she looked over at Frankie and was beaming at the sight of her friend. "Frankie, I'm so glad you're okay! Oh your poor, poor wings. I'm sorry. You know I would never hurt you."

Both Astarroth and Frankie reassured the Princess that she was forgiven and that they all had suffered physical and mental trauma in their collective fight against the Darkness.

Wiping the tears from her face, Ambrosia stood up and looked around the old cabin of her departed friend. She was deeply saddened by the loss of her dear Midnight; the guilt of being responsible was a heavy burden for the Princess.

But yet, she could still sense her friend's spirit was nearby and Ambrosia found it somewhat reassuring.

Depressed and tired, she called out. "Can we go home now?"

Astarroth smiled. "Yeah, let me take care of that."

The Princess yelled, "WAIT!"

She felt compelled to grab Midnight's book of incantations, having the instinctive feeling it was meant to be hers. As well, she tracked down Jade and scooped her up. "You're coming home with me, little one."

This time the cute kitten was very receptive to Ambrosia and they instantly bonded. The feeling was uncanny, but it was almost as if they were old friends. She nodded at the wizard that she was ready to leave it all behind and so he waved his hand in a circle - and just like magic - they were back inside Ambrosia's royal garden.

The burst of sunshine piercing through some clouds temporarily blinded the three voyagers as they had been in the dark for so long.

As their eyes adjusted, they looked up at the majestic castle, the symbolic home of Ambrosia's current reign. But it was more than just a large home with high walls, grand ballrooms, and winding cobblestone staircases. It had been a legacy to the kingdom for generations and offered multiple perspectives and memories.

For Prince Frankie, his shielded memory blinded him from the truth; unaware that this fortress was once his birthright. His devotion to the girl with the rainbow dress was exemplary, but maybe short-lived once the past was to be revealed.

With respect to the acting Monarch of the land, Princess Ambrosia was viewed as a generous, kind ruler with rare magical abilities.

She's now part of Dysterian lore as the one who defeated the Evil Wizard when all hope was lost. Like her little friend, her past is also clouded but her viewpoint on the kingdom is quite clear. She's adamant that she is the rightful Princess and this castle is her home.

With wisdom and experience, Astarroth's view of the castle was far different than most. It was his second home for many years and had many fond memories of watching past Kings and Queens come into age.

But these royal hallways have been host to some of the most vicious and heartbreaking stories an old man could possibly endure. To the wizard, the castle represents beautiful life and tragic death, as well as a mix of harrowing truth and lies that he hoped to finally set right.

But breathing in fresh air, this was a long time coming for the wizard. "Oh, the air is so fresh here. It's great to be back!"

He smiled back at the Princess who joined him in this brief celebration. She released Jade and watched her run free in the gardens.

Still fresh from the shocking news given to him by the wizard, Frankie was not about to let this excitement go away.

"Oh Princess, while you were sleeping, I found out where I come from. I was actually a real person! Can you believe that? And Astarroth and I are going to go on a mission to find a cure. So I can be myself again."

The little firefly was bursting with energy and enthusiasm; however the Princess was taken aback by this bombshell and didn't quite share in his excitement.

The wizard could tell Ambrosia was not as receptive to Frankie's announcement as one might expect coming from a close friend. Maybe it was the thought of losing her little sidekick, or perhaps she was still recovering from the effects of the concussion; but her reaction was less than genuine.

"Oh Frankie, that's wonderful news," she said sarcastically.

Astarroth didn't want this to get awkward, so he interjected. "You know Princess; he's not the only one I can help to recover the past."

This piqued her interest immensely.

"Ambrosia, you mentioned an underground chamber where you found that wretched bear? Perhaps you'd also like to know more about your past; who you are and where you come from?"

The Princess barely waited for Astarroth to finish his sentence, and burst through towards the direction of the secret hatch.

The wizard turned to Frankie, "This won't take long, and then you and I can be on our journey to set you free."

Frankie had never been so nervous in his life, the anticipation of not only learning of his past, but to be human - that would be really special.

The old man quickly caught up to the Princess as they headed into the dark forest. She fearlessly marched through the thick brush as if she was on a mission; she knew exactly where to go. She found the tree she had previously destroyed and the familiar wooden door that started it all.

Astarroth reached for the iron handle, but she dismissed him. She raised her fist, and immediately the door flung open as if it was spring-loaded. Then she quickly produced a simple ball of light and guided it into the hole. Ambrosia really enjoyed her little trick, trying her best to upstage and impress the wizard.

The old man was in awe and admiration of how quickly she had been able to harness her magical powers.

"Oh well done girl! You've been practising." Ambrosia was smug with overconfidence, and brushed off the compliment as if it was nothing.

She descended down the stairs slowly as the dust and dampness started to accumulate around them. She guided her light towards the secret room; it was still open a bit from when she had left it.

The old man spoke up. "Ah, here we are. So Princess, this bunker has been here for quite some time. It belonged to the old King & Queen and was often used to house prisoners. When this heavy door is closed, the room is completely soundproof; which was ideal for when they tortured their captives."

This made Ambrosia shudder.

"But after the horror of your parents' departure, I didn't want you to remember anything. So I hid things - your things - in this room. Your teddy bear, where your mother secretly hid the Darkness, was just over there. That rocking chair; your mother would sit with you late at night when you were a baby."

Ambrosia interrupted. "So you really did live next door to me?"

The wizard continued as he stood in front of the dirty painting of Viktor and Lara. "Oh yes, I may not have told you the whole truth initially, but by the time you were born, the Darkness had already infiltrated your parents; that part is true. And the Ring that I demanded they give back? That was actually my family's ring that your father stole."

The Princess had stopped listening. She was fixated on the creepy portrait of her parents; wondering what they were like. As she recalled the wizard's tale of how he had defeated them, she still had one unanswered question.

"Astarroth. Do you think my parents are still alive?"

The great wizard rubbed his white beard and looked intently at Ambrosia. "It's quite possible my dear, they could be out there somewhere."

The Princess wanted to believe him as she searched the room for other family relics.

He continued. "You know, I'm truly sorry that I misled you and caused you grief when I was affected by the Darkness. But now, I want you to know the whole truth; about you, Frankie, everything. I don't know how you're going to take this, but..."

He didn't get to finish his sentence because he was interrupted by the feeling of cold metal on his arm! The Princess had slapped the other anti-charm bracelet on his wrist. She got up real close to his face and with a deranged look in her eyes - she whispered, "no magic in here wizard!"

The old man looked on in disbelief. "What is this?"

Ambrosia began to smile and trot around the room with glee. "Oh I'm sure you know exactly what that is.

116

You know everything. In fact you know too much. Nobody is taking my kingdom or my Frankie away, especially you! You get to keep your stories and your secrets all to yourself."

Astarroth tried to run for the door, but she knocked him down with some swift magic. He fell against the rocking chair, shattering the antique to pieces.

"Oh, I'm getting good at this magic stuff, aren't I? Anyways, it's time for me to go now. I've got a kingdom to rule. Goodbye Evil Wizard!"

As she began to shut the door behind him, she could hear him yelling. "You can't do this to me; I saved you! I won't tell anybody, I promise. Just take this thing off of me!"

His voice trailed off immediately as she slammed the door leaving him to rot in that musty room. She enjoyed the absolute quiet; knowing the only threat to her kingdom was now forever silenced.

As she reached the surface it began to rain. She didn't want anybody to stumble upon him and risk his escape, so she covered up the door with some nearby branches and leaves and headed home.

Frankie was there waiting patiently to unravel the next chapter in his life, but was confused when Ambrosia came back soaked and alone.

"Where is Astarroth? He was supposed to help me become human again."

The Princess put on a sad face. "Oh I'm so sorry Frankie, I really am. He lied to both of us. We got to the bunker and he showed me all my old things, but then he just went crazy for no reason. He said he couldn't stay in this kingdom any longer and he just vanished. I think he's evil again, I really do. Now come inside, we're getting wet."

Frankie was so devastated and baffled. He really believed in the old man. Could he really be an evil wizard again? It didn't make much sense, but after all the magic he had seen, anything was possible.

Princess Ambrosia led Frankie up to one of the towers that overlooked the kingdom. By the time they were on the balcony, the rain had subsided and the sun began to sneak through.

The view was spectacular and made only further impressive with the addition of a vibrant rainbow that spread across the skyline.

With a hint of an evil smile, the Princess looked down at her little friend.

"Frankie, it's always going to be just you and me, and I won't let anything happen to you. I'm going to be the best Princess this kingdom has ever seen. You and I, we're going to live happily ever after."

The End

www.ingramcontent.com/pod-product-compliance
Lightning Source LLC
Chambersburg PA
CBHW020657180626
46816CB00003B/1322